Short Romance
by
Jackie Lark Gallery

Dedicated to:
The Gang From Something Fishy

Special Thanks to
The Honorable William Murphy
Glenn Hefley
Robert Darr
The Staff at Essex Public Library
Richard Carr

In Memory of:
Mr. Hunter, thank you for sharing those many years with me.

Love Unknown

ONE

"Hey!" The whispered voice had a deep husky sound to it.

Grecia sat up a little, the back of her head pounding with pain. "Why can't I see?" Her voice rose with the panic she was feeling.

"It is pitch black down here." He said, still in a hushed tone.

"Oh." She let out a breath, then asked, "Where is 'down here'?"

"The hull of my ship. More specifically, the gaol." He replied bitterly.

"Pirates?" Her nervousness started again, making her feel queasy.

A chuckle sounded from across the expanse of darkness. "Yes, you could accurately say that." After a shuffling sound, he inquired, "How is it that you happen to be a guest here?"

"I don't rightly know." Grecia stated honestly. "I last remember coming out of a hat shop in the port of…"

"Ahh, you were waylaid." There was no surprise in what he said.

Grecia swore the man sounded thoroughly amused. But, since she did not know him and could not see him, she kept that thought to herself. "Where are your crewmen?"

"Your guess is as good as mine." Now he sounded concerned. "Most of them, hopefully, were on shore leave."

Something in what he said, bothered Grecia. Unable to pinpoint it, she chose to converse further with the man. Talking with someone would ebb the tide of fear in her, if nothing else. She turned her head to the left, where his voice was coming from. "You must be in the cell next to mine." She concluded, since he hadn't come towards her.

"There is only one cell."

As much as it pained her, Grecia stood up and crossed the distance between them. She let out a gasp when she walked into a cold metal barricade. "Where are you?"

A hand caressed her cheek. "Right here, love."

The hand had come from between a set of iron bars. Grecia wanted to be appalled and back away from her captor. Wanted to... Her body refused to move. That one touch had sent an electrifying sensation through every part of her. Her heart pounded rapidly, her breathing escalated. She felt a yearning for something her innocence had yet to understand. "Then, you are capable of releasing me." She breathed out.

More chuckling, then, "My First Mate has the key."

Grecia relaxed, realizing that the problem could be resolved soon enough. "When is he expected to return?"

"Tonight." He brought his hand back to his side. "What is your name?"

"I am Lady Grecia of Winnforest Hall." She knew what the next question would be, but held her tongue.

"And yet, you were without an escort?" He asked in an almost teasing manner.

"I had sent my footman ahead to the carriage with my purchases." She replied indignantly. If this man thought she hadn't heard his mocking tone, then he was wrong. So her next words came with much sarcasm. "It would be *grand* of you to bring a lantern down here."

With a spark and a fizzing sound, the man lit a match. He crouched on the floor, lighting and then adjusting the wick of a lantern. He held it in his hand as he stood and faced her.

Grecia's eyes widened considerably at the sight of the man. Six foot three and muscular, but not bulky. His waist-length hair was the color of chocolate, though the sun had streaked parts of it to a lighter hue. From years on the deck of a ship, his skin had turned to a coppery glow. And his ice blue eyes had a directness to them that breached no nonsense. A black scarf was tied about the top of his head, a small hooped earring pierced into his earlobe. He wore no shirt, only a pair of form fitting dark green pants that were tucked into black leather boots that reached to his thighs.

Grecia deduced that he was a frightening figure to come across, in any case. When her gaze went up again to his face, he grinned. It seemed completely out of place, considering the seriousness of his eyes.

"And you would be?" She barely kept herself from stammering.

"I am Carrian Sopeeri." His hand came up to touch her, but she backed away before he could do so.

Actually, he wanted to touch her hair. He had never seen such a hue before. It was a tan color that hinted more towards blonde than brown. And it glistened in the lantern light. Though held up with pins, one strand had come loose to fall the length of her rib cage. Her eyes looked to be a steely gray. Carrian had not had enough time to be sure of it, before she moved into the dimmer light.

He took a step back. "I will bring you some provisions when I return."

Her mouth dropped open. As much as Gracia did not like the looks of this man, she definitely did not want to be left here alone. "Please." She reached out to him. "Don't go." Just the touch of his fingers, had Grecia breathing strangely again.

Carrian kissed her hand. "I must, so I can send one of the remaining crew to find Costos." At the odd look she gave him, he explained. "My First Mate."

The tingling sensation his lips had caused on her skin, triggered a shiver that ran throughout Grecia's frame. She had been sure that upon seeing the man, he would have no effect on her. Much to her irritation, he did.

Feeling a flush of embarrassment over her own reaction, she stepped away from him. "Then please, be quick about it."

Carrian set the lantern down where Grecia could reach it. "I will be back as soon as possible."

<u>TWO</u>

Grecia stood for what must have been a half an hour. It was when the aching in her head became intolerable, that she finally sat again. With her back leaning against the wall, sleep overcame her.

The heady feeling of floating in the air woke Grecia up. She was being lifted in a pair of strong arms. There was no doubt it was the Sopeeri man, her body was reacting horribly to his nearness.

"Please, I can walk." She moved about frantically, hoping to force him to let her go. It was at that moment that Grecia distinguished what was so peculiar about his eyes. There was a slant on the edges of them. "Are you from the Orient?"

Carrien gave out a low chuckle that had nothing to do with humor. "Persia. Although my mother is from England."

Still, he hadn't put Grecia to her feet. "How did they meet?"

His eyes filled with amusement. "An emissary brought her to my father." With a quirk of his brow, he added, "To be his slave."

"How dreadful." Grecia commented.

"It does have its benefits." He laughed outright this time.

"Not for the woman." Finally he had set her to the floor.

"Oh, my mother is very much in love with my father." He could see a bit of fury in the Lady's eyes. "Did something I say upset you?"

"This ship is moving." Grecia thought to inform him.

"It has been for the last two hours." Carrian led her to the ladder that would take them out of the hull. "Welcome to my ship, Lady Grecia. I guarantee, you will enjoy your stay." Seeing fear in her eyes, Carrean leaned forward to her. "There was such a ruckus over your disappearance in port, that I thought it wiser to drop you somewhere else."

"The northern port would do. I have a cousin…" Her voice faltered at the hungered look in his eyes.

Carrian quickly subdued his thoughts, seeing her react so. He helped her up the ladder and into the main walkway. "Have you ever been to the Orient?"

"No but…" She faced him squarely. "Surely you don't mean to leave me off there!"

"Not unless you so choose." He waited just long enough for her to relax slightly, before adding, "Though that is where this ship is sailing." He took hold of her elbow with one hand. "I think you will be most comfortable in my cabin."

Once inside the room, Grecia wrested free from his grip. "What exactly are your plans for me?"

His gaze traveled over her leisurely. Carrian's body responded strongly to what he saw, too strongly. "We are well beyond the northern port." A husky undertone was added to his naturally deep voice.

His eyes glowed when they finally met with hers. And yes, he had guessed right, those feminine orbs were light gray with just a hint of blue.

Words came out of his mouth before he could even think of what he was saying. "Are you married?"

Grecia's head went to the side as she began her denial, then she stopped. She recalled something about young pure women being worth more to slave traders. A wedded woman had a better chance at being ransomed.

Swallowing hard, she answered. "Yes." What was that look that flashed briefly in his eyes? Regret? Grecia hoped so. But, her reason had shocked her more than this present situation. Shakily, she added, "I have a husband."

Carrian pushed down his initial disappointment. She was lying to him. He almost laughed, a slight grin did touch down on his face. "In two days, we will reach a formidable port. I am sure I can find you safe passage from there." His mind said *'Grecia, come with me'*, though Carrian knew he would not offer that.

"I thought..." She stared at him a moment, shaking her head. "Then you aren't a pirate."

"I have been called that on occasion." He led her past the bed to a large desk with four chairs surrounding it. After seating her in one, Carrian asked, "Why do you question that?"

"I... ah..." Usually able to figure people out, Gracia found herself at a loss with this proposed pirate sea captain. "I suppose it doesn't matter."

Carrian leaned down. One of his hands rested on the arm of the chair she sat on, the other landed high on her thigh. "However," His voice low now, had a bit of a rasp in it. "Until we reach that destination where we will part from each other..."

The words hung in the air. Grecia's eyes closed as his hand moved further up her thigh. "I... umm..." Where that hand finally stopped sent a pulse of delicious sensations through Grecia. Her head fell back as she panted out a few breaths. "No!" She gasped out.

Carrian's mouth came down on hers, sensually. His tongue teased her lips to open. After brushing over her teeth, he sought out the further pleasures inside. When her hand came up to his chest, he steadied himself for her to push him away. Instead, a moan came from deep in her throat. She grasped his shirt, pulling him closer. It was Carrian who broke away from her first.

"Little liar." His eyes sparkled with amusement. "You were to convince me of your innocence and plead with me to send you home."

Grecia could not think as his hand was still moving between her thighs. "Wh-what?"

Carrian stopped what he was doing, a low chuckle emerging from deep inside his chest. "Perhaps the corsairs would have an interest in you."

That one word describing the Barbary slave traders, sent a bolt of shock through Grecia. "But, whatever for? My purity is long gone, I assure you." Her eyes widened greatly as she now realized what he had meant when he called her a 'liar'. "Oh!" Her hand that had gripped him moments before, flew up to cover her mouth. "How did you know?"

He laughed outright at her. "The people who had been searching for you, stated that you had been shopping for your 'coming out' party. Married women don't have those type of affairs."

Grecia let out a laugh of her own, temporarily forgetting her situation. "I suppose that is quite true."

Carrian, who normally was a mass of self-control, now stared at lips that he found irresistible. He gave into that urge and kissed her again. It was no less remarkable than the first one.

THREE

"I still want you." Carrian said to the empty cabin five months later. He swung his legs to the side of the bed as he sat up.

In three days' time, he and his crew had readied the vessel to sail. Without hesitation, he steered them back to where Grecia had first come to be on his ship. As soon as they were docked, Carrian rented a horse and rode to Winnforest Hall.

Dressed in a fine tailored suit, his hair tied back, Carrian knocked at the large white painted door of the manor house. A man with a small moustache opened the portal to him.

"I am Carrian Sopeeri. I have come…"

"For the wedding, of course sir." The doorman stepped aside, for Carrian to enter. A smile touched the servant's lips. "The ceremony has just begun." His hand came up, indicating a door to the right. "I doubt you have missed much."

Carrian almost turned to leave. What could he offer her? Certainly not marriage, for they barely knew each other. After that brief hesitation, he followed the man to the other room.

Carrian leaned in the doorway. The soon to be married couple stood at the other end of the room, their backs to him. The groom looked to be in his fifties. The bride indiscernible under the veil's many layers of lace.

He listened as it was asked if anyone had any just cause… Carrian's hand started to rise as if it had a will of its own. His arm was gripped and brought back to his side.

"What are you doing here?" The hushed voice asked a bit frantically.

Carrian was pulled from the room and into the empty main hall. "I...ah..." He couldn't stop the grin that planted itself on his face.

Grecia giggled in an almost childlike manner. "That is my father, you ninny." Her eyes twinkled mirthfully. "You thought I was the bride! Am I right?" She searched his face, amazed that he was actually standing in front of her. "Why are you here?"

"Could we go outside and talk?" He had been so shook up by the thought of her getting married, that his planned out speech seemed lost to him now.

She looked him over oddly. He was a fine looking man. "Are you here alone?"

Carrian chuckled, understanding her concern. "I have brought no men to carry you off to my ship."

Grecia noted the small disappointment she felt. "Then yes, it should be alright."

They walked side-by-side through the front garden. Carrian gave her an oblique glance. "I have barely slept since you've left." He shook his head at the thought. "I don't understand why."

Grecia came around to where she stood in front of him. "I want to leave."

"Leave?" Carrian had hoped that she would at least hear him out.

"I am not enjoying this husband hunting that society has set me upon." There was a look in his eyes that made Grecia wish she had not said anything. "I would guess you have no appreciation of that."

Again, Carrian shook his head. "Why are you telling me this?"

Her eyes teared up the slightest bit. "I don't know."

When she tried to walk past him, Carrian grabbed her upper arm. "I don't sleep because I want you. Do you think I care to hear about you trying to snare some man to take to the altar?"

Gracia turned her head to smile at him. "You were ready to stop the wedding." She quirked a brow at him. "For what purpose?"

"Because that man was old enough… Carrian laughed. "To be your father."

Gracia leaned against him. "Now who is telling lies?"

"I won't marry you, Lady Grecia." He said bluntly.

"Of course you won't." She looked down at where his hand still clasped her arm. "I think you should let me go."

They stared hard into each other's eyes for a moment. Carrian grinned in such a manner that she actually shivered. "Not this time, Grecia."

"Please, listen to me." Her plea bounced off of brilliant blue eyes that gaged her calculatingly. "I am to stay with a friend next week. She is to have a masque ball."

His gaze remained solid upon her. "What do you expect this to mean to me?"

"I plan to leave from there." She explained. "It was the only way I could find to do so and still be able to take some of my belongings." She was a bit distraught. "I have hired some men to help me…"

"I will do it." Carrian leaned to kiss her cheek. "But I cannot promise you the restraint I had used previously."

She stiffened at the husky sound of desire in his voice. "I simply wanted to inform you, that I will no longer be here." An impish grin slanted her lips. "If I leave your name with the doorman, will you come to the event? To say goodbye…"

His nostrils flared to some extent. "You are not being honest with me." He started walking her back to the manor. "Tell me the truth. Please."

Gracia studied Carrian's face momentarily. Finally, she heaved out a breath. It could do no harm to trust him. "My father has accepted a marriage proposal for me. I do not even like the man. And yet, in two months I am to marry him."

"Cancel your request for aid from those men." He kissed her hand at the door. "I will see you at the party your friend is having."

Grecia was still standing there stunned as he got on his horse and rode out of sight.

The following day, Grecia rode in a carriage to do some last minute shopping. It was later that day that the driver was found bound by ropes, in the stables. By evening, the carriage was found, but not Lady Grecia.

<u>FOUR</u>

"Cap'n!" Costo came running into the galley, stopping abruptly before Carrian. "Tha constable is searching all ships here!"

Carrian cocked a brow at the first mate. "Do I need to concern myself about this?"

Costo looked at his feet guiltily. He knew his captain was referring to the incident of locking a certain Lady in the gaol. "No, all should be secure."

"Double check." Carrian commanded somewhat sternly, somewhat in humor.

Carrian was waiting for the officer at the top of the ramp, when Costo came up beside him. "Everything is as it should be Cap'n."

Minutes later, Carrian walked the patrolman through his ship. "How dangerous is this fugitive you are looking for?"

"Oh no." The constable shook his head. "It is the fair Lady Grecia." He leaned to the sea captain and spoke in a low tone. "It's not the first time this has happened. Personally, I think the chit is spreading her skirt for a lover." He chuckled. "Probably more than one."

Carrian's jawline tensed as he clenched a fist at his side. He let out a slow breath to calm himself before speaking. "Did you want me to open the crates in the hull?"

"No, I'm sure I've looked around enough." The constable winked. "Like I had said, I think…"

Luckily, Costo came up to the two men. He right away recognized the dangerous gleam in Carrian's eyes. "Cap'n?"

"Please, show the constable to the ramp." He said, with teeth gritted. "Then get the ship moving, post haste."

Costo escorted the officer to shore. He set most of the men to work readying the ship as he ran about town to gather supplies. It was in one of the stores that he heard about Lady Grecia. He had known that the captain was supposed to meet with her the following week.

The first mate scanned the other ships that were docked as he made his way back to his own. He recalled seeing one particular vessel and crew that he had dubbed as Corsairs. That ship was no longer in port.

Carrian was at the helm maneuvering the ship through the bay, before Costo had finished relating his thoughts to him.

"But, Cap'n," He swallowed hard. "What if it's not them that have her?"

Carrian's eyes scanned the water. "Tell every man the description of that ship. If it is them, we'll find out soon enough."

<u>**FIVE**</u>

Fear had finally set in. Grecia had waited patiently during her abduction for Carrian to show his face. She had a few choice words in mind to tell him. After three days into the sea voyage, she knew this was not his doing.

For the rest of the trip, she argued with men who either didn't understand her, or refused to acknowledge that they did. It never crossed her mind that these men considered her to be no better than cattle. A livestock to be maintained until it was to be sold.

Her anger had kept the fear away. Now, the dread of her true situation was overtaking her. Once removed from the ship, she was placed in a large room filled with young beautiful women. Grecia was convinced it was a harem she was now a part of. It took her two days to find out that this was the slave trader's hovel.

Men, who she guessed to be princes or other Arabic men of high standing, came through frequently to look the women over. At least, they did that to the women on the other side of the high divider that separated the room into two parts.

Today, one of the burly men who worked for the slave trader, moved ten of the women from the area Grecia was in, to that other side. That isolating wall had been her last sense of security. Grecia was scared. She watched the transactions with fright-filled eyes. That night she got little sleep, if any at all.

When that brawny man came to get her the next morning, she tried to be brave. Grecia was trembling so bad, she could barely walk. By noon she was sold. Sold! To a tall man with dark hair and a beard.

To her surprise, as he walked her out of there, he spoke to her in English. Apparently, he was buying her on the orders of some prince whose name she didn't even try to remember. It didn't matter, for that prince was giving her as a gift to his brother. Of course, the brother was a prince as well.

Grecia wanted badly to be in her own clothing when she was presented to…a sob choked her at the thought… the man who would own her. But, that was not to be allowed, the tall man explained. Whoever she had been, no longer counted here. The man also informed her, that it would be best for her to look straight ahead when the prince looked her over. If the prince did not like her reaction, punishments would be delved out, possible death included.

At the palace of the prince who bought Grecia, she was forced into the care of other women. These veiled ladies bathed, perfumed, and dressed her in what she thought was a ridiculous outfit. It was a wrap of silk that made up the skirt. The top scarcely covered her breasts. A short sheer jacket was worn over that.

When they entered the main room, Grecia snuck a quick glance. They were walking toward the richly dressed men. As they neared them, Grecia caught sight of one prince before casting her gaze downward. He was young, maybe eighteen. She found this odd. It took all her will not to raise her head to see what the other prince looked like. The two princes spoke Arabic to each other for a moment. Then...

"It's alright Grecia, it's me."

Her head snapped up. "Carrian?" He was indeed a prince. And he was furious. She lowered her eyes. "Forgive me."

He chuckled, then said to his brother. "She thinks I am angry with her."

The younger brother laughed as well. Grecia glared up at him. "Maybe brother, you should leave her here for a while."

"I have not decided what to do with her yet." Carrian wondered what her thoughts on that would be.

"You could take me back home." Although relieved by this turn of events, Grecia wondered what her actual situation was now.

"As I recall, you had planned to leave there." Carrian said sternly.

"You should take a wife." His brother suggested.

"I hardly think that to be the solution." Grecia responded haughtily.

The princes glanced at each other, then back at her. Carrian looked angry again. "I honestly haven't decided, Grecia." And then, as if that statement hadn't exhibited his power over her, he added, "You will be gracing my bed, regardless."

"You wouldn't!" Her cheeks flamed red at what he suggested.

With an impatient sigh, Carrian commented flippantly. "I am tired of sleepless nights." He glanced over at his brother. "There will be no missive sent to England."

Grecia's mouth fell open. "But... I..." His angered stare stopped her. She had escaped the lion's den, only to walk straight into the vicious beast's mouth.

Carrian watched her carefully. She looked hurt, yet still so desirable. His voice rasped as he spoke. "Take her to my chambers."

<u>SIX</u>

Grecia sat stiffly on the edge of the bed, staring out the window for quite some time. Finally, she relaxed a bit. This was Carrian after all. He had acted the gentleman with her previously, why shouldn't he do so now? She fretted at her bottom lip. This was a very different circumstance. When something fell on the bed beside her, she was jolted from her concerns.

Her eyes met with Carrian's. "I hadn't heard you come in."

He pointed to the shirt of his that he had tossed down by her. "You can sleep in that, until I am able to get you something else."

"What are your plans for me?" She asked shakily.

"You are frightened?" When she nodded, her eyes wide, Carrian relented. "I thought to hold you in my arms all night. I am not cross with you."

"Yes you are." Grecia observed. "Not because I'm here, of course. That was not my doing. But you are upset because I more or less turned you away back in England."

He grinned. She was acting more like herself instead of the terrified child this ordeal had caused her to be. With a bit of wickedness, he began unbuttoning his shirt.

Grecia openly admired his muscled chest, until she realized what he was doing. "You must turn so I can change."

His eyes widened a bit. "I thought to see what I now own."

Her defenses went up. "You don't own…" His eyes hardened and Grecia realized her mistake. "I suppose you do now."

"I will take you as my wife." He stood, hands on his hips, wearing only a pair of white billowing pants. "The other alternatives, I think you would find less pleasant."

"You could release me." Grecia was sure she could convince him of this.

"You are too wild and seem to easily find trouble." Carrian shook his head.

Grecia gasped out her indignation. "I will not marry you, Carrian!"

"Then you would rather be a concubine." His eyes narrowed. "Or is it the status of a slave that you seek?" As if to himself, he grumbled, "I can't place you in the kitchens. You would likely poison my guests."

Grecia couldn't help but laugh. "What if I promise to always keep a properly armed escort with me?"

The calculating blue eyes turned icy. "Where exactly do you think you are going to go?"

She put a shaky hand to her temple. "Carrian, I can't...stay."

He was trying to be gentle in helping her to adjust. "Then it may be a good thing that the choice is not yours to make."

When she next regarded him, there was a wild, frantic look in her eyes. Carrian silently cursed himself. He had taken the wrong approach with her. And damned if it didn't bring out his male desires to a point of necessity. His need was to possess her, make her know she was his.

"What if you decide that you no longer want me?"

Her voice broke through his thoughts. What she had asked was the furthest thing on his mind. "You may someday feel the same towards me." Carrian shook his head, he had not meant to say that.

"True enough." She then thought more on it. "But, you could take another wife, or sell me. What are my options?"

He cleared his throat before answering. "If you are trying to convince me to take you back to England, you have failed."

"Did you pay those Corsairs to abduct me?" Grecia wondered to what extent this *prince* had gone to have her.

Carrian laughed as he rubbed the back of his neck. "I wish I had thought of that." He paced the room. "But, I really had no plans of letting you know I was anything more than a degenerate pirate."

Oddly, that knowledge relaxed Grecia. "Then you truly had no intentions of making me your wife."

He glanced at her. "My only thoughts were of having you in my bed." A slow grin slated his face, for that was exactly where she was at the moment.

Grecia recognized his expression as a leer. Her eyes brightened. "Then why don't we just have a fling? When it's over, you can take me back to England."

Carrian now knew why his brother had someone other than himself, deal with the women of his harem. It was not going to be easy to condition her, to bury her past. He came to his decision then. Tonight, he would take what she offered. In the morning, she would be placed in his brother's harem, to learn.

"Carrian?"

He turned to look at her. "I can't take you back to England." Why? Carrian knew that he did not want a woman conditioned to be a harem wife. "Damn." He muttered under his breath.

"At least take it into consideration." There was a bit of desperation in her words.

"You will give yourself freely to me?" Carrian didn't like being deceptive, as he was at this moment.

Grecia wasn't sure if she should trust him that far. Before she could respond, he climbed over the bed to where she sat. Kneeling on the bed behind her, he brought her back against his bared chest. His fingertips went lightly down the front of her as he kissed the side of her neck.

"Some men tried to take my ship from me about two years ago." He whispered. "I found out that day, that I prefer to keep what belongs to me."

Grecia swallowed hard. "Do you have a harem?"

"The thought has crossed my mind. But no, I don't have one at the moment." What, he wondered, would be her next move in trying to escape him? "Would it matter at this point?"

"I only asked because your brother has one." She smiled, although nervously. "He can't be but eighteen years old or so."

Carrian's laughter roared. "He is my half-brother and is five years older than me." He added further, "He is thirty."

"What must I do to convince you to take me back to England?" Maybe, Grecia thought, getting straight to the point would work.

Carrian was losing his patience. He eyed the tasseled cord that would summon a servant. It became a distasteful temptation to have her thrown into the harem. But, what if his brother Ghalig thought him displeased and decided to take her for himself?

His hand dipped under her barely concealing garment and cupped a naked breast. "Anything?"

Grecia felt a warm tingling go from her belly then downward. She lost thought for a minute as he rubbed a thumb over her nipple. "Yes." She breathed out.

"Then I will let you know." He withdrew his hand.

Coming to her senses, Grecia asked, "You will let me know what?"

He let out a laugh as his mouth went to the back of her neck. "When you have fulfilled the requirements that would give me cause to take you back."

Grecia suddenly saw herself saddled with two children, dropped off callously at an English port. She pulled away from him, but he drew her back.

"This will not work!" She huffed out.

Amused, Carrian chuckled. "You already agreed." Slyly, he unfastened the sparse shirt she wore. As he moved back, he pulled her along with him to the center of the bed. As he pushed her to her back, he found himself faced with a raging wildcat. She bit, clawed, and hit at him. Carrian pounced over her to keep her from leaving the bed. He had been unprepared for this outburst. In actuality he had expected crying. He carried her with him to the bell cord. While waiting for the servant, her panic worsened. He had her pinned to the bed when a man finally entered the room.

"A sedative." Carrian flung over his shoulder.

"No!" Grecia cried out. "Please Carrian, don't!"

"Shh." He cradled her head to his shoulder. "It will simply calm your fears."

"I just want to go home." She said, attempting to sound in control.

"You did not want to be there." A man and woman came in the room. Carrian kept Grecia's head turned so she did not see them. "What is this aversion you have to me?"

"I don't…" She felt a pinch on her shoulder. "Oh Carrian, I had trusted you."

His heart felt torn as she went limp in his arms. "That may have been a bit too much." He said to the woman who had injected Grecia.

"She will only sleep an hour or so, and be calm when she awakens, Your Highness."

He nodded for the servants to leave, then lay Grecia gently on the bed." *I had trusted you."* Burned into his mind. He had more money and a higher position than whomever she had been about to marry. And, she certainly didn't respond to his advances as if she abhorred him. Carrian concluded that it had to be that the Corsairs' abduction had probably frightened her near to death. He hoped that was all it was.

<u>SEVEN</u>

Grecia woke up extremely groggy and feeling weak. She was also naked and snug against Carrian's body. It did not feel as if he wore any clothing either. Grecia took the one hand she had draped around his chest and moved it slowly downward. Carrian gently grasped her hand and brought it to his lips. His breath was hot as he kissed her fingertips.

"I certainly can't fight you like this." She sighed out.

"Why do you want to fight me?" He moved to his back, holding her to his chest.

Grecia let out a small giggle. "I wish I knew you better."

"Ah." Carrian thought he now understood. "And that frightens you."

"I can't stop hoping that you'll return me to England." Grecia felt so tired, she could barely move.

"You were unhappy with the way your life was turning out there, as I recall." He lifted her chin with a finger and waited for her eyes to open. "What had you planned to do once you left your father's home?"

She made a face of disgust. "I think his new wife has done something to him. He never would have forced me into a marriage on his own."

"Maybe she is drugging him." Carrian suggested.

Grecia snorted out a laugh. "You would get along well with her then."

Carrian chuckled lightly. "I was worried that you would get hurt."

"You didn't... ah..." She didn't feel any different. "Um... while I slept, I mean..."

He found humor in her loss of words. "Will I have to impregnate you in order to get you to marry me? Is that what it will take?"

Grecias laughter rang out. "Are you proposing to me, you degenerate pirate?"

"Hmm." Carrian put a hand to his chin. "I do enjoy sailing. How do you suppose I will fit a harem on my ship?"

Her eyes glistened at his teasing. "Train them to be your crew."

Carrian was glad to see the tension ease between them. "Do you love me?"

"I would not know. I've never been in love before." She spoke as though confiding in him. "I was so terrified, Carrian."

"I know, my love." He kissed the top of her head. "Just don't be afraid of me."

"I think you may be right about my father's wife." She studied the distinctive features of his face. "I wish I could do something about it."

Carrian almost offered his help. Almost. He could lose her if he took her back to England. The British did not take kindly to their noblewomen being sold, even if it was to a Persian prince.

And the solution came easily to him. "Would you do anything to help your father?"

Grecia nearly tensed at his question. But, the drugs were still too strong in her system for that to take hold. "What do you propose?"

Carrian told Grecia what he wanted in exchange for his aid. After that discussion, they slept for a few more hours. When breakfast was brought, so was a milder dose of the sedative for Grecia.

Later that evening, Grecia lay complacently in the bed when Carrian returned. "Is it done?"

"Yes." He said huskily as he undressed.

Carrian slid in between the bedcovers beside her. He kissed her sweetly, then passion took over as he moved his body on top of hers. He did not wait as he pushed his manhood past her maidenhead. A deep groan come from him as her hips rose to meet him.

The sedative had diffused any pain caused by the loss of virginity. What Grecia felt, was beyond her understanding. Her body wanted him to fill her. When he initially hesitated, she thrust herself forward to take all he had to offer. Her body sparked and shattered into a need of sensations that only he could fulfill. Her hands took over, finding the many muscles she had previously craved to touch.

Carrian's mouth went to her breast with moist heat. Grecia cried out as she pulsed and gripped at the beginning of an orgasm. Carrian drove into her hard, losing himself in the heat of her flesh. When she clung to him in the final throes of ecstasy, his control completely vanished and he joined her.

Carrian lifted his head to look at her. "I hope I was able to satisfy you, Mrs. Sopeeri."

Gracia's arms wrapped around his neck and she pulled him close. "If I had known it would be like this, you would have had me much sooner."

"Yes, but," Carrian grinned. "I wanted it close at hand, as only a wife can provide."

Grecia sat up suddenly. Her eyes went over him briefly. Amazement was in her face and voice. "You did hold out until I would marry you. Why?"

"Do you trust me?" He asked with a devilish glint in his eyes.

"Yes." Grecia knew he was up to something and she wondered what it was.

"You must." He deduced. "I could have been lying to you about having a harem."

"Did you?" She lay back, closing her eyes and smiling.

"No." Then hesitantly he said, "But, you will be staying within Ghalig's harem when I go to England to straighten out the mess your father got himself into."

"No, I will not!" She leaned up on her side to glare at him.

"This is not England, Grecia." His eyes glistened like shards of ice. After giving her a light kiss, he continued. "Consider your stay with Ghalig's women an adventure." His tone turned as cold as his expression had. "But, do not get used to that way of life. I have no desire to have a harem wife."

"You honestly won't allow me to return to England." She stated in a resigned manner.

It was a minor show of her beginning to adjust. Enough though, for Carrian to make note of it. "Whatever it is that you are missing from your homeland, I will try to compensate for in your life here. You will, however, remain here in Persia."

"What exactly is the difference between my status as your wife and that of a slave?" She asked, narrowing her eyes.

"Privilege." His own eyes narrowed to slits. "A slave would be beaten for speaking to me as you do. And," He went on before she could say anything. "You can have servants to do your bidding as well." He kissed her cheek. "I own no slaves, Grecia."

"Thank goodness." She then asked what was foremost on her mind. "Why can't I stay at your home until you return?"

"Lovely wife, this is my home." He enjoyed the look of surprise on her face. "My brother's palace was attacked. He is staying here until it is rebuilt."

"That explains it." She surmised.

"Explains what?"

"Why he suggested I stay here." Grecia was coming to understand how much her fears had distorted things.

EIGHT

Grecia woke up to hear Carrian chuckling as he closed the door to their bedroom. She sat immediately upright and stared at him. "You've returned!"

He spun around to look at her. Seeing her so disheveled and barely awake, triggered desire in him. "I docked late last night, but had a few things to take care of."

"Were..." She couldn't help but smile at the carnal look in his eyes. Grecia cleared her throat. "Were you able to help my father?"

Carrian snapped out of the lustful trance he was in and gave her an award winning grin. "That new stepmother of yours is quite attractive for her age."

Grecia felt confused by his answer. Had he betrayed her? When she spoke, her throat felt thick. "She is ten years younger than my father."

His stare became a bit hard towards her. "Ghalig told me of the commotion you started within his harem." He was trying not to smile. "What do you think I will deem as punishment on you for causing such a disturbance."

Her eyes widened. "I merely stated that I did not understand why those women were fighting each other over only one man. After all," Her eyes gave off sparks of rebellion. "There are many good men to be found."

Carrian gasped out in an offended manner. She still did not know he was teasing her. "I can only hope none of Ghalig's women understood what you were saying."

She began to fret, because he still had not told her anything about the situation with her father. What really was her role here? Would he harm her for speaking her mind? Grecia met his gaze guiltily. "I had only spoken to Lasheen." Then in a sing-song voice, she added. "Of course, she was the only one I could talk to... since she was the one woman there who was able to speak English."

"Is she British?" This Carrian already knew. All of his brother's women were from Persia. He wanted to see how far he could drag this out and how honest she would be with him.

"Oh no, she is from here." Grecia tried to smile, though it was meek.

He couldn't hold back any longer. Carrian bellowed out laughter until he was doubled over from it. He barely made it over to the bed to sit by her.

"You have no idea." He could see she was still frightened by what he may do to her. "How hard it was to keep a straight face as Ghalig made his complaint to me." He lay back, putting his head in her lap and looked up at her. "I had to pretend I was angry because he had removed you from the protection of the harem."

Grecia stared at him, her mouth agape. "You are not mad at me then?"

"No." In a laugh, he let out a breath of air. His eyes shone with love and a bit of reservation. "I ah…" He chuckled again. "I met up with your stepmother in town, two days after we docked." He took up her hand and kissed it. "Lovely woman, very generous." Carrian watched her eyes as they narrowed. "She readily admitted to me that I would make much money, if I bedded her." Suddenly they both laughed at the same time. He then sobered. "I did the only thing I could think of, being who I am." He inhaled and then exhaled a slow breath. "I decided that she would make an excellent gift for my uncle, now that he is up in age."

"Oh Carrian!" She exclaimed in shock. "That is not alright! That poor woman!"

"She had asked me if I knew where to get any poison to kill her husband. Apparently, the woman had run out before your father was beyond the ability to mend." Carrian rose up to take her in his arms. "He was bedridden when I first went to see him. I have him here under the care of my physician." He kissed the top of her head. "We had gotten to him in time. It will take a while, but he will heal."

"Does he know I'm here?" She tried to get up from the bed, determined to see her father.

"Yes." Carrien kept his arms securely around her. "He is resting. We will go see him this evening."

She turned her head to smile back at him. "Will you let me up now?"

His eyes became desirous. "I'm having breakfast brought in here. After we eat, I thought…"

She giggled. "I already know what you have in mind."

"I doubt it."

Those three words were enough to frighten her. He was too serious. Hesitantly, she asked, "Then what do you have in mind?"

"I think we should plan a large formal wedding, now that we have your father here." He could swear that he saw mild disappointment in her expression. "Did you think to escape the vows you signed over to me?"

With widened eyes and a surprised grin, she shook her head. "That was the furthest thing from my mind."

Stolen Love

ONE

Sir John Chapton's event was in celebration for his upcoming nuptials. His fiancé, the young Lady Neva of Epping Forest was stunning in her jade green chiffon gown, studded with small diamonds. More of the precious gems adorned her throat and dainty earlobes. At just eighteen, her burnished golden hair in the upswept coif gave her a timeless, almost old-fashioned look. She dazzled the senses of young and old, man or woman.

At thirty-four years of age, Sir John was quite the catch. Never married, he had stayed in service to the crown for twelve years. A very loyal man to those he knew. Six foot tall with light brown hair and blue eyes, he was considered a handsome man. Women had vied for his attention, though he had disregarded that in favor of focusing on his career. He lacked nothing, except to Neva. She was not upset over the marriage, she simply was not in love with him.

After a congenial amount of dances with her betrothed, Neva excused herself from Sir John's company. Her goal was to step outside for some fresh air. Halfway there, a man bumped into her, knocking the flute of champagne from her hand. As the glass crashed to the floor, his arm came around Neva's shoulders to steady her.

"Forgive me. I was not watching…" His dark eyes met with her crystal blue ones. "You look as though you could use some air."

"Yes." Neva nodded, feeling suddenly stifled by all the people in the room. Her hand went to the arm he offered. "Thank you."

Jean Francisco Aldez's other hand quickly pocketed the necklace he had removed from her throat. He led her through the open doors to the stone veranda. They walked to a marble bench by the railing, where Neva sat down.

"I will get you something to drink." He said before leaving her.

Jean Francisco was sure that she had to be the most beautiful woman he had ever seen. He sighed out heavily as he made his way through the throng of people. It would be too much of a risk to stay. She would soon find that worthy bauble of hers missing. Yet, there was so much sorrow in the young lady's eyes.

Neva watched him until he went out of view. She was positive that he would not return. Not after he had so smoothly stolen her jewels. Her hand went to one of the earrings that completed the set. Neva turned on the bench to stare out at the darkness of the estate grounds.

"I thought water may be better if you are feeling faint." Jean Francisco placed the cool beverage in her hand.

"But, I thought…?" Neva scanned over the features of his face. Not the fine lines of aristocracy. More of a chiseled, rugged, masculine look. "I'm not sure what I thought."

"Please, tell me what's on your mind." Jean Francisco knew the game was chancy. But, didn't he live for the risk?

Ah, but he was a suave one, Neva thought. She smiled fearlessly. "I would think it dangerous for a thief to remain so close to its quarry."

Jean Francisco put a booted foot on the bench. He leaned an arm on his knee. "Why are you so sad?"

Not even abashed by the intrusiveness of his question, Neva shrugged. "I somehow saw my life turning out differently."

Glancing over his shoulder to the ballroom, he said, "We will probably have to finish our discussion another day." His long black hair flew about him as a stray wind blew by. "Unless you would like to come with me."

"I doubt abduction is your forte, Mr…?" Neva now saw that Sir John was searching for her inside.

"Jean Francisco Aldez." Without even thinking about what he was doing, his gun came out. "You may be wrong about that." When she gasped, his eyes went to her. "Do not scream, Hermosa."

Neva almost wanted to laugh. She could not have planned a better escape from an unwanted marriage. As he led her down the stairs to one of the many carriages, she felt outside of herself. It was like being a theatre actress on stage. Her situation did not hit her until they were far from the estate and miles on the other side of London.

Jean Francisco extracted the necklace from his coat and held it out to her. "You should keep this."

Neva gave him an odd look. "You may need to sell it, to hold you over until my ransom is paid."

"Then you want to return there?" He asked.

"I thought that is how these kidnappings went." Neva made no move toward the jewelry.

"So your soon-to-be husband is not what was making you unhappy."

"Oh, very much so. But, he is a good man." She watched him re-pocket the necklace.

"How so?" As a thought hit him, his eyes danced with amusement. "You do not love the man."

"Not the slightest bit." Feeling finally free from the burden now that she had spoken about it, Neva relaxed.

"But, he is not cruel." Seeing that her tension had ebbed, Jean Francisco sat back. "What would you do with your life if you had the choice?"

Her eyes lit as the possibilities flitted through her mind. "There are so many things, I simply cannot name them all."

"Well, think on it." He stretched his legs out, crossing one over the other, then closed his eyes.

"I want to travel. To sail off and see other places." Neva said a bit hurriedly.

Jean Francisco's eyes opened just a hair. "A ship is not easy to steal."

Neva laughed. "I hadn't meant..." Feeling playful, she mocked a scoffing manner. "Pirates do it all the time."

"I think that is more than I am willing to take on." He watched her through slitted eyelids.

"How much of a ransom do you think you will get for me?" Neva couldn't see past his thick dark lashes.

He now sat up, giving her a scrutinizing look. "What do you consider your worth to be?"

"I am sure my father would pay well, as long as I am returned unharmed."

"And what of this man you are supposed to marry?" His eyes snapped to hers harshly. "Would he pay more or less than your father?"

"In all fairness, I think my father would be your best bet." She smiled sweetly at him. "Sir John may not believe that you have not defiled me."

"I had not thought about that." He kept his gaze acutely attuned to her facial expressions.

"Yes." Neva let out a breath, casting her eyes to the side. She fingered one of the gems on her dress. "You certainly have done damage to my reputation."

Jean Francisco laughed outright. "And you are no longer so sullen."

"I wonder what I am qualified to do." Her eyes flashed at him. "As an occupation for money."

"If you did not like the idea of marrying Sir John, you would dislike the theatre." He thought carefully for a moment. "If you know many of the modern dances, you could teach others."

Neva made a face at his suggestions. "Both are too common and eventually someone would recognize me."

"Do you ride well?" A picture was forming in his mind.

"I've been told that I do." She gave him a questioning look. "What do you have in mind?"

"Have you heard of trick-riding?" Jean Francisco received a very bland look from her.

"I refuse to become a circus act." Neva turned her nose up in the air.

"I wasn't implying that you should." His gaze became intense. "Do you think you could learn the maneuvers?"

"Why yes, of course." She responded with certainty.

"What do you know of weaponry?" He was more sure of his idea now.

Her shoulders drooped, but in a seemingly forced dramatic way. "Very little."

Jean Francisco crossed over to sit beside her. He leaned so close that his lips touched her ear. "I am not convinced." Feeling his own gun jab into his side, he hesitated. Jean Francisco put his hand over the one she held his pistol in. "How will this benefit you?"

"It will free me from you." Her eyes narrowed. "You have the necklace and I have a tarnished virtue." She threw back her head and laughed. "I highly doubt that unless it is true love, that any man will enjoy involvement in my scandal."

"True, but…" He looked up at the carriage ceiling. "How do you plan to get past Armand once we are stopped?"

"I can't imagine him jeopardizing your life." Neva jumped over to the seat opposite of him. "Especially since you did gain the jewels."

"You don't know Armand." He said under his breath. Then louder, Jean Francisco said, "Let's hope you are right."

A cynical brow raised on Neva's forehead. Studying him further, she was sure he was speaking truthfully. As if on cue, the carriage slowed to a stop. Neva saw fear in Jean Francisco's eyes.

"Here." With a shaking hand, she gave him back his weapon.

After holstering the gun, he opened the door and stepped outside. Jean Francisco lifted Neva from the transport. A huge burly man was already standing there. His hair, eyes, and clothing were all black. A very formidable sight to come upon, for anyone.

"This is Armand." Jean Francisco put a hand out toward the hulking man. "My brother."

Neva's eyes burned with hostility into her captor. "You told me, that if he saw me with your gun…"

Armand's stare swung in her direction. "I would have shot you in the head."

Neva's posture weakened considerably. "Me?" When he nodded, her gaze went to Jean Francisco. Her mouth opened, but no words came out.

Jean Francisco lifted her in his arms as her knees gave out. "Never again, soldado." He looked at his brother. "Put out a ransom demand."

"Ransom?" Armand showed much surprise at this news.

Jean Francisco nodded. "Make sure they cannot trace it back to us."

"All this for money?" Neva said, still dazed.

Jean Francisco's face came down right in front of hers. "Money has nothing to do with this."

As he started walking, Neva looked at their surroundings. A large home, built cottage-style seemed to be where he was taking her. "How can a thief afford this?" She asked, as they passed a beautifully chiseled statue of a mother holding a child.

"I would guess you do not know how much your jewels are worth." He carried her up the stone steps and into the entry hall.

"The set with the earrings cost thirty-five thousand pounds." She saw his disbelief. "That was when my grandfather bought them as a wedding gift for my grandmother."

In the front parlor, he lay her on a settee. He removed her earrings before propping a pillow behind her back. "I will put them in my safe. They will remain your property."

Neva closed her eyes once he left the room. She wondered what would truly become of her after she was returned to her parents. What if Sir John still wanted her for his wife? Now, more than ever, she did not want that marriage to happen. Her parents might even send her away to a convent.

A few tears trickled from Neva's eyes. It was so unfair. This man talked to her of true freedom. So soon, it would be taken away from her.

Jean Francisco brushed the wetness from her cheeks. "Have I caused this distress?"

"I don't want to go back." Neva rolled over to face away from him. She cried like a child while hugging herself.

"It is alright." Jean Francisco turned her back toward him. "It's your choice. You can do whatever you like."

"B… but, you…? The ransom!" Fresh tears flowed from her as she became desperate.

"I have no intention of collecting it." A sternness came over him that he seldom used. Jean Francisco was angry at himself, for causing her anguish.

Neva leaned up on an elbow. After wiping at her face in an attempt to regain her composure, she asked, "Then why do that?"

"They will be looking for a woman who has been kidnapped. Not one who is wandering around freely." He gave her an off-handed grin. "That way you do not have to fear discovery."

"What do you want for helping me with this?"

"There are many things I want." He did not know what to make of her sudden shift into submissiveness. "But, none of them are a condition of you gaining your independence. I am in a position to help and have a desire to do so."

Neva's eyes went to his and she found warmth there. She could not recall the last time she had seen that in anyone. "How old are you?"

He laughed, the previous stress leaving from the simplicity of the question. "I'm twenty-four." His gaze went over her form. "How attached are you to that gown?"

Neva looked down at it and grinned. "Not very much. It reminds me of a grave mistake I almost made." She yawned. "There are ninety-one diamonds sewn into it plus seven larger ones embedded in the clasp."

"We will sell them." He put a hand out for her to take. "Then, you will have money for whatever you wish. Come now, we should sleep."

Neva froze where she stood. "Sleep?"

"Yes." Jean Francisco turned to face her. "I have no ambitions of forcing myself upon you. Though tonight, you will be staying in my room with me. However, tomorrow you will have your choice between five rooms to make your own." He laughed lightly. "There is one that is connected with my suite. You may want to stay there, until you feel safer here. And once I am sure it will not be used on me, I will give you a gun."

<u>TWO</u>

The furniture in his room was made of rough-cut wood. Curtains, bedding, and one upholstered chair by a writing table were done in a thick black satin. It made the light color of the oaken wood stand out. If not for tapestries hung on three of the walls, the room would have been shockingly bleak. Instead, it showed a bold masculinity that made Neva blush.

She turned to Jean Francisco. His stare was so intense upon her, that she had almost forgot what she had been about to say. "I will need something to sleep in."

He went to a dresser and pulled out a pair of his pajamas. "We will find something for you as soon as possible." As he handed the clothing to her, he added, "After you have settled in here, I will teach you trick-riding." He could see she was about to protest. "If anyone asks, we will tell them you are my student."

"That was very sneaky of you." Neva understood though, acting was not her best quality. This would prevent her from having to do so.

He pointed her to a curtained corner. "You can change in there." His eyes were affixed on her as she moved away from him. "Lady Neva?"

She stopped and faced him. "Yes?"

They stared at each other for the longest time. "I hope you choose to stay."

"Why would that be, Mr. Aldez?" She assessed him quickly and wondered how much she should trust him.

"I think you would be happy here." Seeing her yawn again, Jean Francisco flicked a hand in the air. "Hurry now, we both need sleep."

To his surprise, Neva ran to him. She planted a light kiss on his cheek. Jean Francisco's hands wrapped around her upper arms. He stared deep into Neva's eyes. As he bent to kiss her, she moved her head away. With a grin, he captured her lips with his own. Her hand came up to slap him, his own rose up to stop her. Their hands intertwined in the air.

Jean Francisco let out a loan moan as Neva took a step away from him. When the kiss ended, their eyes stayed locked on each other. There was a mutual unspoken vulnerability between them. With their hands still clasped together, Jean Francisco brought her to his side. Releasing her hand, his arm went over her shoulders. He walked over to the curtained off cubby.

After an hour of Neva tossing about in the bed, Jean Francisco moved her up against him. "Try to sleep, Dama."

"I don't know what is wrong with me." Neva felt restless, when she had been exhausted just an hour ago.

Jean Francisco sat up, dimly lighting the lantern on the nightstand. "You have never been taught about desire?"

"I know nothing of that." She let out a breath in a huff. "This is very…"

He cracked a grin. 'Frustrating?"

"Yes." With wide innocent eyes, she smiled. "And no."

"Let me help you." He lay on his side, facing her.

Neva grabbed at his hand as it went down the pajama pants she wore. She gasped out when it touched down between her thighs. She stopped struggling against him when his finger slid inside of her. It felt too good. A small cry escaped from her as his lips found hers. She seemed oblivious to anything other than where his hands and mouth touched her. And there was very little of her body that he did not explore. When his mouth replaced where his hands and fingers began, Neva lost control.

Her fingers tangled in his long ebon hair as she pulled him closer. "Jean, no God!" She called out, barely aware that she had done so.

Jean Francisco stopped long enough to look up at her. Hearing her say his name in the throes of desire made him ache for her. He knew that would have to wait. Driving her further into a wantonly state, his own self-mastery was sorely lacking. Jean Francisco bought her into a breathless orgasm. His mouth traveled back up until it met her lips again. The kiss she returned was warm and passionate.

After some minutes passed, Neva felt out of sorts. She thought to joke off her nervousness. "I could always go back and marry Sir John, then keep you as a lover."

In a moment's time, he was over top of her. His eyes were that of a feral animal. "Or, you could marry me." He kissed her in a wild manner, holding nothing back.

"I could never do that." She saw his questioning look. "My parents would not give consent."

"You would let that stop you, if you were in love?" Jean Francisco knew he was taking a chance with the question.

"If that were the situation, I would try to wait until I were old enough to make the decision myself." Neva realized that if she stayed with Jean Francisco long enough, she could make the choice on her own.

As if reading her mind, he said, "You could do that here."

"Yes, I suppose that's true." She laughed. "Except here, I have you to withstand."

"Ah, so you would not think to become my wife." A devilish grin matched the sparkle in his eyes.

"I am not in love with you." Her laughter rang out at his feigned look of dejection.

"I have an offer to make you." He waited long enough to see her curiosity come forward. "You stay here one week with me…"

"It could do no harm." Neva knew there was more to it though.

"Then, I want you to leave, or try to." Jean Francisco felt the shock of the risk go through his chest. "If you can go, you can return any time you like. But," He took up one of her hands and kissed it. "At the end of that week you *will* try to leave."

"That's all?" She then thought further. "What are we to wager in this endeavor?"

This time Jean Francisco laughed. "What do you have to wager?"

"Not much." She was enjoying this gambit.

"Do you think you could ever love me?"

"Anything is possible." Neva answered. "But I would not think something so important to be put to a test."

Jean Francisco's hand ran down the side of her body. She responded with a sigh. "Just try to leave me."

"Oh, you do not play this game ethically." Neva said after coming to her senses.

"Do you want to leave?"

"No."

They both laughed. Jean Francisco moved off of her. Soon, they both fell asleep in each other's arms.

THREE

"Neva."

She opened her eyes slowly. A stunned look came upon her face. The previous night she had simply been too afraid, to notice how handsome Jean Francisco really was. His stance had more confidence in it than any man she had ever known.

"Oh!" She moaned out. "You will never let me leave!"

"Do you love me? He asked.

"Of course not." She replied, moving to the side of the bed furthest from where he stood. She sat upright, a fearful look on her face. "What if I do leave in a week, and someone finds me?"

"Then I would guess..." His expression became undefinable. "You will marry Sir John and take a lover."

"I can't live like that." She wrung her hands nervously. "What do I do?"

"Then you wait and I will come get you." His features softened. "Or, you could stay here."

"No." She caught on to his trickery. "I think I will have to disguise myself."

"That is something I can help you with." He walked around the bed, to stand near her. "I will show you around the grounds. After you pick a room of your own, we will remove the gems from that gown." He winked at her. "I was joking last night, there is no reason for you to leave in a week." He handed her a thick robe. "Let's go eat."

"I think…" She glanced at him as they walked from the room. "Well, it may be too risky for Armand to set out with a ransom note."

"He left early this morning." He lay his arm lazily across her shoulders. "Armand will be safe."

"I would rather not leave until my disappearance is not so fresh in people's minds." Neva paused halfway down the stairs. "I don't want to return there."

The room she chose was indeed the one that was connected to his. Jean Francisco had pointed out that they could share meals in the joined sitting room that was set between the two suites. It was decorated in a simple manner with a small table, two chairs, and a settee made from maple. The fabrics were light green with gold thread running through it in small pin stripes.

She also had a beautiful view of a large pond. It was surrounded by apple trees and weeping willows. The scenery was ethereal. And, Neva soon found out that the entire grounds were as well. More scatterings of willow with their draping branches swishing in the gentle breeze prevailed on the grassy terrain amidst multicolored wildflowers. Here and there mimosa trees with their blushing pink and white flowers brought a softness to the vista. The morning carried a mist of fog that added to the charm of the terrain.

At the stables, a building of dark brown painted wood with white trim, Jean Francisco brought out a long-legged mare. Her coat was a light golden shade, almost white.

"This is Cabal." He stroked the mare's neck. "She will be your mount."

Neva looked her over. "She is a fine breed."

"Your lessons will start next week." He laughed at the brow she raised. "I expect you to be here."

"I do hate to lose a bet." She defined playfully.

"I will keep that in mind." His voice was low, throaty with desire. "We should start extracting those gems from your dress."

Neva took one of his hands in both of hers. "You cannot tell me that you afford all this on token acts of thievery."

A shrill whistle had both of them looking toward the homestead. Armand was standing outside, waving an arm in the air. Jean Francisco tied the mare to an outside post. Together, they walked to his brother.

Armand's face was grim as they approached. "Four of Elpert's men were on the north hill. They rode off when they saw me."

"There is no access to the land from there." Jean Francisco's gaze traveled across the terrain they were speaking of. "I wonder what they were doing."

"Watching." Armand stated outright. He nodded toward Neva. "We have to be careful with her."

"Did you get the message through?" Jean Francisco asked as the trio walked inside.

"I gave it to Charlene, after telling her what was going on." The large man grinned. "She's going to pass it through her girls and eventually to Dense Morgan's Gentleman's Club."

"Is that where he goes?" He glanced down at Neva, who was doing her best to follow the conversation.

"He has a fondness for a girl named Millie, who works there." He too, now looked at Neva. "Word has already spread across London of the missing heiress."

"Heiress?"

Neva cringed at the look on Jean Francisco's face. It was a grimace of severe distaste. "I should have told you." She said quietly.

"This will be hard to avoid for quite a while." His eyes ran down her body. He had obtained a peasant skirt and blouse for her to wear, from the housekeeper. "I doubt those men would have guessed who she is." Giving her a light kiss on the cheek, he said, "I will go put your horse up. Bring the gown to the parlor, so the three of us can take it apart."

FOUR

Neva and Armand were carefully cutting the diamonds from the fabric of her dress, when Jean Francisco leaned in the doorway. Both looked up at him, their jaws fell in shock. Every part of his body seemed to have blood on it. He dropped to his knees where he had stood a moment before. Two men came up behind him.

Armand reached for his side-arm. His hand froze as one of the men pointed a gun at Jean Francisco's head. He was the one who spoke. "We're here to return Lady Neva to her home."

"I've been here two days, sir," Neva wasn't the only one surprised as the voice of a true American southern belle rang from her vocals. "And there is no Lady Eva on the premise." She looked at Armand in question. "Or is that the name of one of your finely bred horses?"

The man with the gun wouldn't have been convinced except that she had gotten the name wrong. "No, young lady..."

"Miss Natalie Cobalt." Neva smiled while batting her eyes flirtatiously. "Mr. Aldez here..." She put her hand out toward Armand. "Knows my father. They apparently thought it would be amusing to have me tutor under Mr. Aldez's brother," She waved a distracted hand in the air. "Some sort of special riding ability." A grateful smile curved her lips. "On which, I believe you have temporarily relieved me of, with your brutality towards my instructor."

The man looked down at his feet in embarrassment. He nudged the man beside him. They each took ahold of one of Jean Francisco's arms and brought him to his feet. After setting the injured man in a chair, he turned again to Neva. "I'm sorry if this caused you any inconvenience."

"Oh, no." She gave him a great big smile. "I assure you gentlemen, the delay is a pleasurable one for me."

After the men left the room, Armand went to a window. As he watched them leave the property, Neva went to Jean Francisco.

"My lord! Are you hurt badly?" She moved aside his blood soaked hair to look at his face. To Armand, she said, "Get some soapy water and towels."

Once they were alone, Jean Francisco took Neva's hand. "I was wrong. You are quite the actress." His voice came out gravelly. "You did not seem afraid."

Neva started to comment, then realized he had passed out. She and Armand cleaned him up before taking him to his room. Armand then left to fetch a doctor. She paced the room a few minutes then sat on the bed beside Jean Francisco. His eyes remained closed, though his breathing was steady.

Neva leaned down, kissing him on his brow. "I was very afraid… for you." Taking one of his hands, she held it to her heart.

He squeezed her fingers, whispering to her hoarsely. "I will be alright, Neva."

It was not long before Armand returned with the physician. Neva went back down to the parlor, to allow the doctor to do his work undisturbed. Louisa, the housekeeper was just finishing up with cleaning the blood spilt from her employer.

As she rose from her knees, she gave Neva a consoling look. "This was not done because of you. They have done it before to Jean, and Armand too. They are bad men. You being here was just another excuse for them to attack."

"But, why do they do it?" Neva wasn't sure if the woman knew who she really was.

"The land, it is what they want." Louisa shook her head as she picked up the bucket and scrub brush she had used. "First they burned all the vineyards, then the cattle slowly came up missing." She let out a mournful sigh. "Senior Armand was supposed to marry a lovely lady from the homeland. She became too afraid to come here." Her expression became thoughtful. "I suppose you will leave as well."

"I have no intention of letting those vulgar men scare me away." Neva's chin came up in stubborn pride. "I may just go to the man they work for and give him a piece of my mind."

"You'll do no such thing." Armand stated adamantly as he entered the room. His gaze went from one woman to the other. "Jean Francisco and I decided that if any of those men come on our property, they are to be shot."

"Then I will need a gun." Neva felt a coldness in her that had not been there before.

"I think my brother has two set aside for you. He is resting now, I will ask him when he wakes up." His eyes followed the housekeeper until she left the room. Armand laughed a little. "She will make sure everyone on the grounds knows what to do with those men."

"How badly did they hurt Jean Francisco?" She couldn't shake the feeling of guilt over what had happened to him.

"He'll be walking around in the next day or two. Most of the blood you saw, was not his." Armand grinned wide, then winked at her. "He had beaten two of the men unconscious, before he was taken down."

"Then they were the four men you had seen earlier." She almost laughed, her relief was so great.

"Yes." His eyes went to the gown she was working on. "I wondered if you would mind sitting with my brother until I return." He scooped up the loose diamonds that had been placed in a glass bowl. "We have a man in London who buys from us. I will take Louisa with me to make purchases for you. She will know better than I, what needs you may have." He paused at the doorway. "There is a gun in Jean Francisco's writing desk. Enrico will be outside the house, keeping a watch. He is about my size, with a scar on his right cheek. If anyone else enters the house and it is not him, do not hesitate to shoot."

Neva nodded, taking up the dress and empty bowl. "Could you have Louisa set out a strong broth and bread? I am sure Jean Francisco will be hungry when he wakes up."

"I'll do that. Anything else you can think of?" Armand's view of the spoiled aristocrat he thought her to be, had completely vanished.

"Yes, if there is perhaps a boy about my size…" She surmised. "I would like to borrow a pair of breeches and a blouse from him."

"I'll have those for you before we leave." Armand gave her a nod then stepped from the room.

Neva took her things up to Jean Francisco's room. To her surprise, he was awake. "Are you hungry?" She asked, setting the gown and bowl aside.

"No." He said in a dispirited manner.

Neva thought of what Louisa said about Armand's lady. She thought maybe Jean Francisco guessed her to be of the same weak demeanor. She let out a laugh. "Armand has set me here to protect you from further abuse."

He brought his arm up from where it had lain at his side. A gun was held in his hand. "I am sure he meant it to be the other way around. I'm not so badly hurt that I can't defend myself."

She went to his bedside. "Then what has you so concerned?"

"Those men know you are not being held against your will." Jean Francisco closed his eyes tiredly. "If you are found, it will go bad for you."

"At least it will keep you from a hanging." Still, she worried. "Maybe I should go back. I could say that I escaped from my abductors." Her head went back as she laughed. "And then, I could say my kidnappers were those same men who did this to you."

This prompted laughter from Jean Francisco. He winced, as it caused his injuries to throb painfully. "Alright, I will eat." He sat up weakly. "In the top drawer of my dresser is a small gun. Put it in your pocket."

Neva went across the room. Before she reached the dresser, Armand came in the room. He handed Neva the garments she had asked for. After receiving them, Neva took the clothes along with the gun and left the room.

Going into her own room, Neva changed quickly into the boys clothing. Instead of going to the kitchen to get Jean Francisco's food, she went into the joined sitting room. Neva listened at the door leading to his suite.

"She is very frightened for me." Jean Francisco said.

"I was thinking that it may be safer for all of us to go to Spain." Armand could be heard pacing the room. "For a year, until her situation quiets down."

"She would have more freedom to do as she likes there." He groaned out as he moved around.

"I didn't tell her that you had been shot." Armand looked out a window. "I'm sure she didn't see your leg when we were cleaning your wounds."

Neva went hastily downstairs before they noticed she was gone too long. She thought about Spain and then other places away from England. No matter where she went, she would be noticed. And, wouldn't that be even more likely in another country?

"She is a stronger woman than she looks to be." Armand saw now, that his own Ophelia hadn't had the aptitude to endure the problems here.

"I should have taken her." Jean Francisco had much to fret over now. "She is used to being around gentry."

"All the more reason for us to go to Spain." Armand grew quiet when Neva brought a tray of food in. After saying his goodbyes, he took his leave.

Neva propped pillows behind Jean Francisco's back, so he could sit up properly to eat without difficulty. Seeing how weary he looked, made her feel bad for eavesdropping.

Worse, was the decision she had made. "When Armand returns, I will be going back to my parents."

"Why?" Jean Francisco asked bluntly.

She hung her head down. "I think it would be best for all of us.'

He gaze had that untamed look again. "Do you love me?"

Her eyes came up to meet his stormy stare. "I do not know."

"Then maybe it is possible that you do?"

She shook her head. "I don't see how that can be. I had only met you last night."

"When Armand returns, we will all be going to Spain." Strong desire burned in his eyes. "You have no reason to go to your parents. Or am I wrong?"

Neva knew at that very moment what her feelings were. None of it made sense, but that didn't matter to her. "There is a strong possibility that I am in love with you. Though I don't know how it happened."

"I do." He searched her face for some clue of deception. "It's the same reason I picked out that mare for you. Take her on a ride tomorrow, you will see what I mean."

"I don't know if I can do this, Jean." Her eyes pleaded with him. "It's too hard, knowing what I do."

Regrettably, he knew what she meant. "You do not think you can adjust to this life." Slowly and painfully, he rose from his bed. "Follow me."

Limping across the room, Jean Francisco waved for her to come with him. He threw open the window he stopped at.

Once Neva came up beside him, he grinned. "There is freedom and choice out there." His voice was throaty, sensual. "Come to Spain with us. If you don't like it, you can come back to whatever life you choose."

"I can do that." She gave him an odd look. "But, before I do, I am going home to get some of my things."

"I wish you wouldn't." Jean Francisco took her in his arms. "Armand and I will go with you if you do." He thought further. "You should let us go inside to get whatever you need. We are more practiced at that type of thing."

Neva glanced up to see him grinning. "I could tell you what I want and where it is."

Much fog and misting rain welcomed them, as the trio approached the properties surrounding the mansion. Neva had insisted on going with, in case the dogs were loose on the grounds. Luck was with them, since the curs were secured in the stables. After tying the horses in a thicket of trees, they crept onward.

Neva took the two men to the east wing and pointed at two windows on the third floor. "That is my suite." She led them to a small door in the far end of the building. "All the rooms are empty on this side. You will go past four doors on the left, before you reach mine."

Jean Francisco held her close, kissing her amorously. "I want you to go back to the horses and wait for us. If we are gone too long, you are to go here" He handed her a folded note. "He is a very good friend of ours." After another kiss, he and Armand disappeared through the door.

Neva leaned against the door a minute, then headed across the lawn. She put a great amount of distance between herself and the mansion before passing in front of it. Twice, there was a sound to her left. The fog was too thick to see anything, so Neva quickened her steps. She was suddenly hurled to the ground, the air knocked out of her lungs. Neva went unconscious.

<u>FIVE</u>

A week later, the two brothers sat at the breakfast table. "Look at this!" Armand slapped the London daily news circular down in front of Jean Francisco. "One hundred thousand pound ransom demand for the return of the missing heiress!"

"So, she did not return to her family." The younger Aldez man said glumly.

Armand tapped the headline with a finger. "I had only asked for fifty thousand pounds in the letter I sent to Chapton. There has not been any mention of that yet."

"Maybe he has not received it yet." After staring at his food a moment, he pushed the plate aside. "Or maybe it is a play to flush us out."

"What if Elpert's men followed us there?" Armand had strong doubts that Neva had gone off on her own. "They could have taken her."

"We can take a look." Jean Francisco said half-heartedly.

"I sent Enrico to watch Sir John's London townhouse, and Lon is at the Chapton country estate."

Jean Francisco was staring out the window, barely hearing his brother. "I don't think it was Elpert's men."

"We should at least take a look."

Turning quickly to face Armand, Jean Francisco glared angrily. "She is not there!" He picked up the newsprint then slammed it back down on the table. "Who would benefit from her never being found?" His words echoed through the room.

"A relative." Armand answered calmly. "Whoever would inherit if she were..." He didn't complete the thought, couldn't actually.

"Dead." Jean Francisco finished. Both men looked at each other, not wanting to believe the possibility. Jean Francisco cleared his throat. "We need to find out who that is."

The old castle was mostly dilapidated. One wall on the north was all that stood. The dungeon however, was intact. It had been made somewhat functional. Two rooms had been turned into bedrooms, with thick pallets on the floors. Another, had a small fire-pit for cooking and crates to sit on.

"I don't understand why you are doing this." Neva sat on a pallet, hands tied behind her back. She had tried the ropes binding her, but there was no give in them.

His eyes glistened a bit insanely. "I am going to get what I want. Only this time, you won't be able to stop me."

"This one." Jean Francisco waved the missive in the air. It was one of the many they had read that had come from the carved letter box brought from Neva's parent's home.

"Who is it from?" Armand had separated Neva's correspondences into three piles. The first were from a female cousin of hers. The second were some love poems, lacking passion and creativity. The writer of those was unknown. Third came from a friend of Neva's, whom she had known in finishing school.

Jean Francisco grinned. "Cousin Annabelle. She writes that if the man is that disgusting, Neva should say something to her parents. Otherwise, the man will be in her life for all eternity."

"Sir John?" Armand let a shudder run through him.

"I would guess." He read further. "It doesn't say, so it could be anyone."

Lady Annabelle sat in the parlor as the two men were escorted into the room. She put a hand out to the settee across from her. "Please gentlemen, be seated."

"Thank you, for seeing us." Jean Francisco said, though the lady's eyes remained on Armand.

After taking in the sight of the massively muscular man, Annabelle's gaze went to the other one. "You said this was concerning my cousin Neva. Have you seen her?" She smiled, then corrected herself. "Since the disappearance."

Armand brought out the letter Annabelle had written to Neva, along with the sordid love letters. He handed them to the seemingly unusual woman. The soft reddish hair and light blue eyes made her look delicate. Yet so far, she acted far from that description.

Lady Annabelle looked first at the correspondence written by her own hand. She made a face after a glance at the other letters.

She stared steadfastly at Armand. "To what purpose have you brought these here?"

Her first instinct told her that these men were Neva's kidnappers. Something else though, she couldn't quite define, led her to believe she should trust these men.

"We have reason to think that whoever has her, is not wanting mere ransom." Jean Francisco's eyes went from his brother to Lady Annabelle. He choked back a laugh at the love-struck look both of them had. Coughing loudly, he continued. "We are going to search for her."

Annabelle's attention snapped to the smaller of the two men. "Then I am going with you."

Jean Francisco's brows went up. "I do not think…"

Her elbows rested on her knees in a very unladylike manner, as she leaned forward. Calmly, she said, "Well, I think I have loved her for much longer than you, sir."

Two very stubborn sets of eyes locked together, then turned to Armand as he laughed heartily. "We're trying to be discreet. I think your family will notice if you are gone for any length of time, Lady Annabelle."

"My parents are in Morocco until the end of the season. And my brother chose to stay at the academy during their break. You see, I am quite alone here."

"I have a question that may be far from what we're looking for." Jean Francisco still thought otherwise though.

"Please go ahead, Mr. Aldez."

"Jean Francisco." He stated before nodding toward his brother. "And he is Armand." Continuing, he asked, "Who inherits next in line after Neva?"

"I do." She answered.

"Not your brother?" Armand queried.

"No." She sat back, folding her hands in her lap primly. "He is my stepmother's child. Both she and my father have been previously widowed."

"Then who is after you?" Jean Francisco felt they were now onto something. It was obvious the inheritance came from Annabelle's mother's family.

"There were only mother and Uncle Morris." She scanned her memory. "I think I recalled my mother mentioning an uncle of theirs." Her eyes lit with recollection. "Yes, he had four or five children. They ended up very poor off, for he had a gambling problem."

"That's it." Jean Francisco then inquired. "Do you know if Neva or her parents kept up with that brood?"

"No. I mean, I'm sure they hadn't." She eyed the ridiculous love letters. "Hubert Avery was a bit of a worm. I don't know if he had the nerve to do something to Neva though."

An idea came to Armand. "Did your mother have a family bible?"

"Yes." She smiled at the man who had her heart racing. After ringing a small hand-bell, a servant entered the room. "Bring me the bible on my nightstand."

Minutes later, Armand had the book in his hand. He paged through the births and deaths. His eyes went to Lady Annabelle. "Woodrow Stents?"

"Yes, that sounds right." She went over to stand beside him.

Jean Francisco looked over his brother's arm to the page. "One of his sons had a boy whose name was Avery." He pointed to the entry. "He would be twenty-two years old now, and is the oldest."

Annabelle gasped. "Hubert is the same age."

"I think we need to see if we can find him." Jean Francisco's expression was dangerously dismal. "His plan is to kill Neva and you as well, I am sure of it." He could not bring himself to think that Neva had possibly been murdered already. "Do you have an address for this man?"

"Oh, he won't be there." Annabelle was sure of it. "Though I suppose we should stop by to be certain." Her eyes twinkled with a bit of anger. "I do know what property they had left after everything else was taken from them. That is most likely where that wretch would take her. It is the remains of a castle, with no one around for miles."

"Where is it located?" Jean Francisco rose to his feet.

"Did my cousin leave her engagement celebration willingly, or did you force her to go at gunpoint?" Her shrewd gaze went from his holstered weapon to his face. "If you will excuse me, I must change into suitable clothes, for the long ride we have ahead of us."

Jean Francisco's hands clenched at his sides as she flounced from the room. "She is purposely trying to bait me." He turned to his brother and scowled. "You should convince her to stay here while we go."

"I doubt she will do that." Armand was grinning from ear to ear. "I have an instinct that Avery plans to keep Neva alive until he has Annabelle as well."

"Do you think he's doing this alone?" He knew his brother's uncanny intuitions were strangely accurate.

"Of course he isn't." Annabelle said upon entering the room. She had quickly decided on wearing one of her stepbrother's riding outfits. It was a little big, but more functional than anything she had. "He most likely has a few others that have fallen from Woodrow's rotten tree." Her hand flicked towards herself. "Follow me, gentlemen. We will surely need to arm ourselves more properly."

Annabelle took them into what she called 'The Game Room'. It was filled with many stuffed and mounted animals from all over the world. Two large glass cabinets took up the far wall. They were mostly filled with an assortment of guns, as well as a variety of other weaponry.

She brought out ten of the firearms, each accompanied with spare ammunition. "Try not to lose any of these." She said while handing all but three of the guns to the men. "My father has great pride in them."

"We need to get going." Armand felt a strange chill.

Annabelle stared both the men down. "How did that beast get ahold of Neva anyhow?" She walked them out the back door to the stables.

"We had snuck into her parents' house to get some of her things." Jean Francisco shook his head at the memory. "He had taken her while we were inside."

"She was with you?" When he nodded in answer, Annabelle laughed lightly. "What were her plans after that?"

"We…" Jean Francisco let out a breath. "I don't exactly know."

"Well, I can tell you what they were." Annabelle set the men to saddling two of the horses. "She has been trying to get away from her social obligations for a long time. You taking her that night, couldn't have worked any better for her than if she had planned it herself." Her eyes locked on Jean Francisco. "Have you bedded her yet?"

Armand chuckled quietly over the woman's boldness.

"No." Jean Francisco was becoming irritated by Lady Annabelle's constant questioning. He felt a small satisfaction in seeing the surprised look on her face.

"Oh, you really are done in, then." She smiled at him, kindly this time.

"What do you mean by that?" His eyes narrowed.

"You are ready to chase after a lady who is in dire straits," She mounted one of the horses. "And yet know nothing of what the outcome will be with her."

Holding the reins of her horse, he asked, "Do you know?"

"I think we will all find that out soon enough." She said in seriousness.

The group stopped at the flat in London that Avery had rented. As Annabelle had thought, he had not been there for a week. After buying provisions for the journey, they headed north. It was a four day ride on which they were able to find inns to stay at. Finally, the towns started giving way to open land.

Annabelle reined in her horse as they crested a hill. "The castle will be just over the next rise."

Armand pointed to a thick woodsy area. "We can go there until tonight."

"I'm going to go out on foot, to see what the layout is." Jean Francisco said as they dismounted in the cover of the trees. "And to see how many people are there." He looked at his brother and nodded before leaving.

<u>SIX</u>

The scene that unfolded before Neva was too familiar. Two of Hubert's cohorts came in the room, half dragging a bloodied man. They dropped the man to the floor in front of Hubert.

The taller man who was called Edson, spoke. "Found him wandering around out there. He said his horse threw him."

Hubert looked at the man doubtfully. "Has anyone seen this horse of his?"

"No." This came from the one named Wilk. "But his clothes were muddied and he seemed a bit dazed when we first saw him."

"Tie him up, until we know for a certainty why he is here." Hubert's gaze went to Neva. "Is he anyone you know?"

She shook her head.

"Not in your class of friends, huh?" Hubert sneered.

After the men had the stranger securely bound, they left. Hubert went out with them. Neva was not sure if Jean Francisco was conscious. His hair had fallen in front of his face and he did not move.

Taking a chance, she whispered. "Gone."

His head came up, his eyes immediately going to hers. "I love you, Neva."

"Armand?" She asked in a hushed voice.

"And Annabelle." He watched, but saw no surprise in her expression over that.

"Good lord, you must be prepared for a war!" Her heart did a flip when he grinned and nodded.

"Tonight."

They became quiet when Wilk came into the room. He glanced at the injured man who lay on his side, apparently passed out. Kneeling before Neva, his hand went up her thigh. She tried to move away from him, until he put his knife to her throat.

"Avery said we'll each have a turn at you tonight. Be nice to me and I won't hurt you too much." His eyes narrowed coldly. "But there will be pain."

Annabelle stomped up to where Armand rested against a tree with his eyes closed. "Your brother didn't take any weapons with him. It's almost dark and he has not returned."

He looked up at her nonchalantly. "I'll bring the guns to him. And don't worry, he should be with your cousin now."

Annabelle sat down beside him. "I think we should approach the castle from two different directions."

Armand gripped her chin. His eyes searched hers as he shook his head. "I want you to stay close to me, where I can protect you."

"I am as good a shot as any man." Her chin lifted high in the air.

"Then you can protect me." Armand laughed a moment, then became serious again. "We may have to leave in a hurry. It would become a problem if one of us lay injured alone out there." He kissed her without a thought. "Why haven't you married yet?"

"I have." Annabelle watched his face drop. "And was widowed within a year. It was a freak accident. His carriage went over a cliff."

"Unlikely." Armand said softly. "When had your mother passed away?"

"Four years ago." Annabelle eyed him nervously. "Our London townhouse caught fire. She was the only one there at the time. That is, other than the cook, who also died."

"It sounds as though Stents' offspring have been removing your family from their way, one at a time."

Annabelle broke into tears at the thought of her mother and husband dying over other people's greed. Armand held her as she sobbed over the loss of those she loved. He kept her in his arms until it was time for them to go.

"Look! Over there!" Edson pointed at the dark shape moving swiftly by the castle. He and Avery rode out to it.

A half an hour later, Avery kicked at the bound man on the floor until he sat up. "What does your horse look like?"

"A dapple roan with a black saddle." Jean Francisco held his hands behind his back. In them was the rope that had bound them together.

"We have him." Avery paced the floor in front of his captives with a pistol in his hand. "It's a shame you had run upon us though."

Before Avery could bring his gun up, Jean Francisco swung his legs across the floor. Avery's feet were kicked out from under him. The gun slid to where Neva sat. As Avery reached for it, she slammed her heel down on his hand. Avery started to yelp in pain. That was cut short when Jean Francisco knocked him out cold. He untied Neva's hands and then both of their feet. He used the ropes to bind Avery.

Taking up the gun, he handed it to Neva. "Stay close to me. We will try to get to Luminar." He grinned back at her. "My horse."

As soon as they were outside of the castle. Jean Francisco let out a low hissing sound. The stallion came right up to them, soundlessly. He nudged Jean Francisco with his nose. After lifting Neva onto the roan, Jean Francisco mounted behind her. Just as silently, they rode away.

When they had made some distance from the ruins, Jean Francisco whispered. "I wonder where the other men are."

They rode in a wide circle around the place. Neva laughed as they rounded the back of the castle. Wilk and Edson were both on the ground hog-tied. Armand and Annabelle waved them over.

Annabelle smiled at her younger cousin. "They haven't harmed you, have they?"

"No. Though they were planning to." Neva turned her head to see Jean Francisco's face. "Now I'm going to have to go home. It is the only way to be sure those men are imprisoned for what they have done."

"Imprisoned? No mi amor." He held his arm straight out to his side. "Armand."

The other Aldez man threw a pistol to his brother. Jean Francisco caught it in the air. Bringing the horse up in front of the bound men, he fired twice. Each of the shots went into the heads of Neva's captors. She turned to look away as he kicked the horse. They stopped in front of the castle ruins. Jean Francisco dismounted, bringing Neva down beside him.

"Condenar!" Jean Francisco cursed under his breath as they entered the room they had left Avery in. It was now empty of people. The ropes that had held the scoundrel, lay in the middle of the floor.

SEVEN

Annabelle handed the letter to be delivered to Neva's parents, to Armand. It explained everything from who Hubert Avery really was, to an embellishment of Neva's kidnapping. She also maintained that Avery was still running loose. Annabelle added that Neva and she were both safely hidden at a friend's ranch. She stressed on the necessity of secrecy, until Avery was caught.

"We are going to Spain." Jean Francisco announced at breakfast a week later. He had noticed a tenseness in Armand, had felt it in himself as well.

Annabelle looked up at the younger Aldez man. "I thought the plan was to lure that bugger Avery, into a trap."

"The men here know what to do." Jean Francisco took hold of Neva's hand. His eyes grew intense on hers. "I want you to marry me."

They had boarded the small ship that would take them across the Bay of Biscay to Spain. The foursome stayed at the rail as they watched England fade from sight. With nothing more to see, the group turned to go to their cabins.

He stood there, shaking his head. Each of his hands held a gun pointed at them. Avery gave out a disparaging sigh. "I really thought you to be smarter than this, cousins."

Jean Francisco could see that the other people on board had gone below to their rooms. The nearest crewman was far enough away that he most likely wouldn't hear any gunshots.

"You are insane with greed." Annabelle retorted angrily. She hoped to keep the reprobate's attention on herself. "A coward, to be sure."

This made Avery laugh. "That could be possible, but I'm soon to be a wealthy coward."

"Hah! The authorities know who you are and what you are up to." She claimed scornfully. Then, just to get him to continue talking, Annabelle asked. "How did you get loose back at the ruins, anyhow?"

"That is the beauty of it, dear cousin." His grin was sadistic. "Who do you really think your lovely stepmother is?"

Annabelle's eyes grew with rage. "What have you done?" Armand grabbed her back to his side as she started to go after Avery. She struggled uselessly against the large man. "You better pray that God forgives you if you have done anything to my father!" She spat at him. Tears streamed down her face, but they were angry tears.

Jean Francisco used the distraction to bring his gun out. He aimed his shot at a knee, knocking the thug off balance. As Avery fell, his weapons flew off in different directions.

Jean Francisco knelt by the man, his gun pushed against the bony scull. "Where are the other two? They are your mother and brother, I am guessing."

Avery grimaced in pain, but refused to say anything. Armand's beefy fist met with the scamming murderer's temple. Avery was knocked out cold

Armand glanced over at Jean Francisco. "Go tell the captain to turn this ship back to England."

"We will compensate him greatly." Annabelle added.

"I wonder if they have done anything to my parents." Neva looked at Annabelle. "Those assassins were right under your roof the whole time."

"I can't believe Jimmy had anything to do with this." Annabelle said about her stepbrother. She wasn't quite sure, but something didn't feel right. Her eyes went to Armand. "But he had to know who Avery was."

Armand too, had a gut feeling about it. "I have a doubt that he and his mother had part in this. But, there is someone else missing."

Jean Francisco returned to find Armand lifting Avery over his shoulder. The brothers took the man to Armand's cabin, where they were to wait for the captain to come speak with them. Neva and Annabelle stayed in the adjacent cabin, keeping the door open between the two rooms.

The captain listened to the men, then went in to talk with the women. He did not doubt their story, for he had heard about the missing heiress. He readily steered the ship back to the port they had just left. It would not delay him that much, England had barely been out of sight.

EIGHT

Upon Grant Mandall's illness, the trip to Morocco had been cut short. Sharice Mandall was disappointed…somewhat. Back at the manor, they ate a light dinner before Grant made his way to the bedroom. Many aches and small shooting pains went through his body as he hefted himself up the stairs. He supposed that was old age creeping up on him.

"Darling," Sharice smiled at him. "I will bring a nice pot of hot tea for you shortly."

He nodded wearily. "Maybe a snort of brandy with that would be nice."

Sharice made sure he got into bed, before she went down to the kitchen. As was usual at this hour, the servants had all gone to bed. She put the water on the stove to boil. Still, she looked around the room apprehensively as she put arsenic in the empty pot, then added honey to disguise the taste.

"I didn't want to believe it."

She turned around with a gasp. "Oh Grant, you frightened me!"

"Annabelle had a missive sent as soon as she heard we were here." He pushed open the door to the hallway, letting the constable into the room. "You should be ashamed of yourself, involving your sons in such treachery."

Sharice knew it was over. She didn't fear going to prison, it would never happen. "*Jimmy* knows nothing about this."

"Avery has been caught, my dear." Again, he shook his head. "And with Jimmy so bright and ambitious."

Calmly, she said. "I told you, Jimmy knows nothing about this. It was all Avery's idea."

"Are you going to tell me that Jimmy doesn't know his own brother?" Grant thought something seemed very wrong with her, other than her being a murderess.

"They are not brothers." She stated simply. "When my husband died..." She laughed somewhat insanely. "I should have been left well off." She looked now at Grant. "Instead, he left everything to his only child from his first marriage. Oh, we had it planned so well. She was young and we made it look like she was killed in a robbery." Sharice sighed. "It was too easy, I should have known."

The constable crossed himself. He had never encountered anyone who had committed such horrendous crimes as this woman was confessing to. He walked over to the back door to allow his men to come in.

Sharice took the small folded parchment from her pocket and carefully opened it. She poured the remaining contents into her mouth. Swallowing the powder was not easy without something to chase it down.

In his shocked state, it was a moment before Grant realized what she had done. His attention went to the back door, where a group of officers were lining the far wall.

"She just poisoned herself!" He said as the door behind him opened.

"Father!" Annabelle came up behind him and gave him a hug. "Thank goodness…" She looked about the room. Her eyes narrowed on Sharice. "You wicked woman! We have sent officials to go get Jimmy as well."

Grant put his hand up, to hush his daughter. "Jimmy is not involved. I will explain it to you later. I think, I will need Dr. Matthews here before the night is out."

Annabelle left her father briefly to go outside and talk to Armand. After giving him directions to the physician's home, she went back in to stay with her father.

Neva and Jean Francisco stayed at an inn near the port. She wanted to go see her family to make sure they were alright, but they were to wait here until word came from Armand. Neva did not fully understand why they were to stay here, but she trusted these men.

It was not until the next morning that Armand showed up at the dockside room. He was so tired, he barely comprehended why his brother and Neva were looking at him so anxiously.

His eyes went to Neva. "Sharice is dead, she took the poison she had been giving Annabelle's father. Grant is going to be alright. The physician left just before I did. I stopped by your parent's home to let them know what happened and that you were alright. I explained that you were not to return until we were sure that everyone involved had been caught."

Neva nodded. "I suppose that they haven't gotten Jimmy yet."

Armand's eyes widened. "Jimmy was apparently Sharice's previous husband's son. He had nothing to do with any of Avery's debauchery. Although Sharice, had been quite involved." He went over to the extra bed in the room and lay down. "I will be ready to go after I get some rest."

Neva looked to Jean Francisco. "Go where?"

The younger Aldez man gave her an odd look. "To Spain."

"I don't really see a need…" She almost laughed at the matter-of-fact look he gave her as his arms crossed over his chest.

"Do you love me Neva?" He was more than sure that she did. It was more important that she acknowledge it, for herself.

"Of course I do." She gave Jean Francisco a look that told him she thought this was no grand secret she was revealing.

"We will stay in Spain until you are old enough then." He considered the matter done with.

"Old enough for what?" She batted innocent eyes at him.

He grinned. "Old enough to decide to become my wife."

Her eyes shone with humor. "Are you proposing marriage to me?"

Jean Francisco growled, though he was far from angry. "Yes."

"Ah… I wonder if I will accept." She moved a little away from him as she recognized the lust in his eyes.

Jean Francisco glanced away from her. "You will."

"I wonder how legal it would be if we married as soon as we arrived in Spain." She went over to the bed they were to share and lay down.

"There is no one there to tell us that we cannot do that." His head went to the side, as he tried to decipher if she was teasing him. "Is that what you want to do?"

Neva patted the bed beside her, for him to join her. "I think it would be a wiser choice than waiting."

Jean Francisco just stared at her for a few minutes. "Will you marry me, Neva?"

She smiled. "Yes."

To Love The Wild Heart

<u>ONE</u>

Manny Hedder scanned the passengers as they disembarked from the 'Larauli'. He was sure she was the pale young lady who walked alone in the second group that came ashore. In her correspondence to him, she had stated that he would recognize her by the dark plum dress she wore. Manny guessed that the purple colored outfit on this woman, must be the one. He made his way through the throng of people.

"Ah, Miss Caspin?" When she nodded at him hesitantly, he smiled. "I'm Mansfield Hedder."

"A pleasure to finally meet you." It was an honest answer. At her youthful age of twenty-five, a man of forty years was expected to look old. Not this one. He was built stocky, muscular, but no taller that five foot eight or so. His blond hair showed no graying. And his brown eyes, though plain, showed none of the fatigue that came with age. *'This will not be so hard.'* she thought to herself. Taking a step toward him, she extended her hand. "Elizabeth, please."

Taking the offered hand, Manny walked them both back to the ship. "I will arrange to have your trunks brought to where we are to meet the coach. Then we can go to the courthouse."

Still tired from the long voyage from England, and a bit overwhelmed by this new *'America'*, Elizabeth allowed Mansfield to lead her from one place to the next. She nervously gripped her overnight bag, as the man who was now her husband opened the door to their room at the inn.

"We have five hours before the stage leaves." He explained, whisking her through the door.

No sooner had that door closed, than he started stripping his clothes. After watching Elizabeth slowly remove her own garments with shaking hands, Manny moved them to the bed.

There was no prelude, no words of love as he stretched over top of her body. She was a mail-order bride, it was as simple as any business deal.

Unprepared, Elizabeth yelped out as he shoved himself inside of her. After ten minutes of prodding in her and pinching her breasts, he was through.

Manny poured water from the pitcher into the wash basin. Wetting a cloth, he brought it to her. "There will be blood."

Elizabeth stared out the window of the coach. It was the second day of the five days journey to Manny's ranch. The scenery went from fields, to woodland, then back to fields. A glimpse of a river or stream now and then, broke into her line of vision. She wanted to cry, but could not. Instead, an empty feeling filled her entire being.

For four years she had helped in the children's nursery at the Bellis home. The position ended when Mr. Bellis suddenly took notice of the young Scandinavian nurse-maid. It was almost a relief when Mrs. Bellis caught her wayward husband trying to drag Elizabeth into one of the bedrooms on the second floor. But, it had been Elizabeth who had been blamed. Mrs. Bellis made sure her disgust with the hired girl was heard in every decent household within her status.

Elizabeth's reputation was ruined. It was by chance she had found out about a service that supplied wives to men in different countries. Within a month's time, she had been placed on a ship headed for America.

Elizabeth was jolted out of her thoughts by men shouting outside of the stagecoach. There were gunshots heard, then the carriage took on a dangerously fast pace. Mansfield gave her hand a squeeze as he brought his gun out from its shoulder holster. Elizabeth sized up the two men sitting across from them.

The one was maybe twenty and dressed in his Sunday best. She guessed him to be a student traveling home from some university. The other man was portly, wearing a fancy suit which appeared to be quite uncomfortable. An expensive looking gold chain peeked out from his vest's watch pocket. They were thoroughly frightened. *'Both of them will be useless if a fight arises.'* Elizabeth surmised.

The coach stopped abruptly, throwing those two men to the floor. Elizabeth gaped at the people outside. Deeply tanned and wearing only buckskin pants. There were ten of them. They were bald except for a strip of hair down the middle of their heads. That was trimmed short, so it stuck straight upward.

"Damn!" Mansfield said. "Mohawks."

The elder of the two men gasped. "What do we do? They'll kill us!"

"Let me handle it." Mansfield went past Elizabeth to open the door. "Follow me out slowly."

Elizabeth was the second one to leave the coach. The younger man was the third to step into the sight of the doorway. The sharp retort of a rifle was heard and Mansfield Hedder crumpled to the dirt. Elizabeth stared in shock as the other two male passengers were killed. She was still standing frozen to the ground as the natives began plundering the contents of the coach. A hand fell to her shoulder and she jumped.

"You will come with me."

Elizabeth flung herself away from him, but not far enough. His hand reached out and clamped on her wrist.

"No!" She cried out in a strangled scream.

"You keep quiet. You do not fight me and I will let you go when I am done." There was no further resistance as he pulled her behind him to a grouping of small bushes.

Elizabeth said nothing. This was the man who had shot Mansfield. She prayed her fate would not end the same. When he pointed to the ground, she immediately sat down. He shook his head slightly, though his eyes never left hers. The native unlaced the front of his pants before kneeling in front of her.

He brought out a knife, which he quickly put to her throat. "Not one sound from you." He spoke quietly, pushing her fully to the ground.

Elizabeth clenched her eyes closed and nodded. She felt him push her dress up before her undergarments were torn away. Once he was in her, he moved slowly.

It was far from unpleasant as she felt the full length of him. Elizabeth let out a small gasp. His hand brushed her cheek lightly. Elizabeth opened her eyes and found herself staring into the dark eyes of a man who was bringing her to the pleasure of womanhood. A battle of emotion went on inside of her.

He watched her face as his hand unbuttoned the front of her dress. Her eyes studied him until he gently caressed her bared breast. When her lips opened, his mouth touched down to further confuse her thoughts.

He continued his pace as her body clenched around his in orgasm. He had known right away that she had been with a man before. But, he was sure she had never experienced the climax of desire he had brought her to.

Elizabeth lost all concept of time as the native had his way with her. What he did was intense and felt so good at times, that she wanted to cry out from the indulgence of it. But the most this man would hear, were the sharp intakes of breath or an outburst of exhaled air. She lost count of how many times he had taken her to these extreme heights. He was ever gentle, as a lover should be. And when it was over, she wished it wasn't.

He still lay half over her, his fingers running over her breast. "You could stay with me."

"You killed my husband." She was so calm, she could have commented on the weather in the same tone of voice.

"Maybe my brother will like you."

No sooner had he said that, when one of the other native's came to stand a few feet away from them. The man stood there with a grin, then moved further away.

"You said you would allow me to leave when you were done." She couldn't seem to raise her irritation more than the smallest bit. And she was mesmerized by this man, seemed unable to stop staring at him.

He drew his gaze away from her momentarily, as if in thought. Then, giving her a light kiss, his eyes brightened before becoming serious. "Come with me." Before she could speak, his finger touched down on her lips. "Shh. The others are ready to leave. It is not safe for you to stay here alone."

Another of the natives walked by, shaking his head as he chuckled. He re-buttoned her dress, then stood, bringing her up with him.

"You could take me to the nearest town." She looked over at where the other natives were gathered in a group. "Or allow me one of the coach horses, so I can go there myself."

He swung her around to face him. "I did not say I was done with you yet."

He strode to where his brother held his horse. Only his eyes showed amusement as he could hear her following close behind him. He whipped around fast, grabbed her by the waist and set her atop of his horse. Just as quickly, he leapt up behind her. The natives left at a fast pace, their horses racing at top speed.

TWO

Dawn was barely visible when they entered the Mohawk village.

"In English, my name means 'Night of Light'." He whispered as they rode quietly past a large arc-roofed building.

"My name is Elizabeth." She glanced around as they stopped. They were now in front of another building that was about half the size of the first one, the structure identical.

He slid off of his horse. "This is the village of my people." After helping her down, he added, "It is where you will stay until I am done with you."

"And when will that be?" She was unable to read his expression in the dim light.

With a grunt, he handed his horse over to his brother.

After leaving her in the care of an older woman, he said was his mother, the native left. For three weeks, Elizabeth helped in the gardens, cooked, cleaned, and spent time tending to the young children there. She did not see him in all that time.

Two things happened that she was grateful for though. A pair of the younger natives had one day brought to her, the trunk containing her possessions. A week later, to her relief, her womanly cycle came. Neither man had gotten her pregnant. Three days ago, that had ended. Elizabeth determined to confront the native the next time she saw him. She did not, however, see him enter the building just before the dinner hour.

Night of Light's gaze went to his mother. With a big grin, she nodded to her son. He left the building without a word.

Elizabeth lay down in the soft pelts, on the bunk where she slept each night. A few people were talking at the other end of the longhouse. With desperate thoughts of how to convince one of the natives to take her to a town, she dozed off. She awoke an hour later, when Night of Light climbed over top of her.

"Shh, Elizabeth."

Her hands came up to push him off of her. At the touch of his bare flesh, she recoiled as if burned. There was no time for further thought as he entered her. Her body came alive under his caresses. He lifted her hand to his lips, then ran his mouth down the inside of her arm.

Bringing his head up next to hers, he whispered. "Let me have you, Elizabeth." When her arms wrapped around his neck, Night of Light let out a breath and closed his eyes.

He came to her nightly, then would leave before the sun rose. A month went by, then another. There was not an evening that went by that he didn't go to Elizabeth.

One morning, just before breakfast, Night of Light came in and looked at his mother. She shook her head and grinned. Suddenly her eyes widened. It was too late. Elizabeth poured a bucketful of icy stream water over his head. Many of the women in the longhouse started laughing. Night of Light didn't care. He grabbed Elizabeth by the waist and swung her in a circle. Elizabeth squealed as he lifted her high in the air.

"Put me down!" She finally spat out.

He did, placing a hand on the flat of her stomach. "Our child is there."

Elizabeth was stunned. She had buried herself in her duties and lost all sense of time. There was no reminder here of what month or day it was.

"A baby?" She asked meekly.

He saw her tremble and took her in his arms. "Our baby." He walked her outside.

"You said I could go." She said quietly.

"You are still angry at me for killing your husband." He took her along one of the woodland paths.

"I barely knew him." Elizabeth felt a burden leave her just from speaking about it. "He…" She stopped, seeing the odd look on his face. "What did I say wrong?"

"You didn't love him." He seemed astounded by his own words.

"No, of course not." She did not like the look in his eyes. "Why?"

"Do you love me?"

"I think I am beginning to." She noticed he was pleased by the answer.

It was not that he smiled, she had yet to see him do that. Though, the harshness of his face had left and his eyes glistened. And then, he let out a laugh.

His whole face lit up as he leaned toward her. "I am one of the most feared warriors among the Mohawks. I have never frightened you. Which is good, because I have not wanted to since the day I first saw you."

"I want to talk about you allowing me to leave." Elizabeth had to say it, before she again became too amazed by him to bring the subject up.

"No." He gazed off in the distance. "It will never happen, Elizabeth. I think there is enough love between us, that we can be honest about it. I don't think I will ever have a reason to let you go."

At first she did not understand his mood and why he would not look at her. Then it occurred to her, how simple it all was. "You are in love with me, aren't you?"

Night of Light nodded, a genuine smile creasing his face. "Yes." He glanced at her. "I love you, Elizabeth."

"That does not leave me much hope." She said tiredly.

"I know you like what we do together." He laughed a bit, his eyes taking on a feral gleam. "I will hunt you down, if I am given no choice. I think you like it here."

She shrugged. "It is so very different here."

A scream was heard coming from the village. After a moment, there were more, from many people.

Night of Light grabbed her by the arm. "You wait here for me."

Elizabeth lifted her skirts to catch up with him as he went up the path toward the village. "No!" She called out softly.

Night of Light had turned to tell her to go back to wait for him, when shots were heard. He waved her back instead. Elizabeth nodded, then quietly left him.

THREE

It was well into the afternoon when everything quieted down. Hearing some riders approach, Elizabeth hid behind a fallen tree. When they stopped and dismounted, she peeked out to see them. It was two American men. With them was one of the young Mohawk women. Elizabeth knew her, had helped her with her two year old son.

The woman was gagged, with her hands tied in front of her. Her eyes went from fear to anger as the men grabbed at her, tearing her clothes. When they shoved the woman to the ground, Elizabeth stood up.

"What is it, you men are doing here?" She asked in her most authoritative voice.

"Never, you mind…" The larger of the two men turned to face her. "Sorry miss…" His expression became suspicious. "What're you doing out here in these woods, anyhow?"

Elizabeth let out the loudest, shrillest scream she could, then took off running. The man who talked to her gave chase. Elizabeth ran a full circle around where the other man held the Mohawk woman. While evading the one who came after her, she continued to shriek. Two shots were fired and both men fell to the forest floor.

Elizabeth ran to the woman and removed the gag from her mouth. After several tries to untie the rope that bound the woman's hands, Elizabeth let out a frustrated breath.

Two deeply tanned arms came around either side of her. In one hand was a knife that cut through the binding cord. The young woman spoke quickly in the Mohawk language, to Night of Light. His arms wrapped around Elizabeth, hugging her to his chest.

"She said you are a very brave woman, and that you care deeply for our people." He kissed her ear, growling out. "If you ever do anything that puts you or our child in danger again, I will beat you." He felt her shaking and leaned around her to look at her face.

Elizabeth could hold back no longer, and burst into laughter that was caused mostly by relief. Night of Light smiled. He had not been joking, or at least he thought he wasn't. This was the first time she had laughed since he took her from the stagecoach. And, she seemed incapable of stopping it. His grinned widened as she made futile attempts to regain control over herself.

After taking in and letting out a huge breath, words finally sprang from Elizabeth's mouth. "You will not beat me."

His voice was deep by her ear. "Yes, I will."

It was enough to sober Elizabeth completely. "You would hurt me?"

"If it will keep you from worse harm or death, yes." When she struggled to be free from his embrace, he did not relent. "I will be careful not to harm the child."

When her laughter rang out again, Night of Light released her and stood. The more menacing his look became, the harder she laughed.

The Mohawk woman didn't know what to think of this odd display. Night of Light looked thoroughly enraged. Why wasn't the white woman afraid? She glanced timidly from one to the other. Rapidly she told Night of Light that his woman was reacting to the fright she had earlier held in.

The warrior shook his head, pulling Elizabeth to her feet. "How am I supposed to beat you, when you become this way?" His face was stern as he spoke through clenched teeth. He kissed her roughly. "My blood runs hot, seeking you to cool it."

When he made love to her that night, it was in a crude, rugged manner. Tormenting, then pleasing her, his hands and mouth went over her body.

Keeping quiet was nearly impossible for Elizabeth and a hushed moan or two did escape her. Nothing stopped him, until he had taken her fully and she clung to his body in agonizing rapture.

When he moved away from her, Elizabeth's body felt internally bruised. He had made his mark on her and seemed satisfied at her body's need to stay near to his.

As he moved to his side, Night of Light reached back to bring Elizabeth closer to him. "There is no other place for you to go, She Wolf. So, do not ask to leave."

"I love you, Night of Light." She whispered.

"I will hunt you down if you leave me." He glanced back, but could see nothing in the darkness. "And I will beat you." He sighed. "I doubt even that could make you fear me."

"I assure you, that if you find me gone…" She burrowed closer to him. "I had not left by my own choice."

Night of Light whipped around to cradle her in his arms. "I hope we have a daughter."

This surprised Elizabeth. Most men wanted their firstborn to be male. It was a sign of their virility. "How odd."

He chuckled quietly. "She can then help you with all the sons we're going to have."

As she giggled softly, he lifted her lips to his. The kiss was so gently and loving, it brought tears to Elizabeth's eyes. "You called me a she wolf." She chastised.

"You do not like the name you were given?" He then said *she wolf* in the Mohawk language.

"My name?" Elizabeth had to admit to herself, that the foreign word made her feel good. It may have been the love and pride Night of Light displayed when he said it.

"You will learn more of our words."

THREE

The attack on the village motivated a need to secure the forest that surrounded the Mohawks. A band of the natives left on the trek to ensure their safety. They did not want to be surprised again. Elizabeth watched as Night of Light led the group away.

Two days went by and Elizabeth despaired that none of the people left behind could speak English. On the third day, a lone native rode into the small village. She had never seen this man before.

He was maybe ten years older than Night of Light, wiry, yet muscular. His face was thin, with prominent cheekbones. The dark eyes were hard, mean, and angry, yet sharp. This native reminded her of an eagle or a hawk.

He walked past where Elizabeth was toting a basket of laundry toward the stream, and into the smaller of the two buildings. Elizabeth continued on her way. She soon lost herself in the task of cleaning her clothing.

"You should have clothes like the other women here."

Startled, Elizabeth turned to the voice. "I am not so sure I can ply a needle through deer hide."

The native held out a soft, light tan, buckskin dress. "Jumping Fox wants you to have this." He took two steps closer. "She told me what you did, when those men had taken her. Thank you for helping my sister."

Elizabeth accepted the dress with a nod. She watched as the native's features relaxed into a grin. "What do they call you?"

"Whispering Eagle." He brought out a small knife, placing it in her hand. "I have been scouting out the land around us."

Elizabeth thought he would leave her to her task. The native sat down on a nearby boulder. "Would your sister wear one of my dresses, if I gave her one?" She tried light conversation, for this native made her quite nervous.

"She said she likes your clothes." He nodded, again smiling.

"Good. You can help me pick one out for her." She laughed when his eyes widened in fear. Elizabeth laid the garments out for him to see. "Which one?"

He pointed to a peach frock. "That one."

This time Elizabeth smiled. "It will go well with her darker skin." She began scouring the garment, then glanced back at him. "I would guess that you have many things to do." She prompted, in hopes that he would leave.

"No." With that simple statement his eyes stayed steadfastly on hers.

"Surely, you don't mean to sit here and watch me." Her irritation sounded clearly in her voice.

"Yes, I do, Elizabeth." As calmly as the man sat, his senses were ever alert.

Her shoulders slumped as she turned back to her washing. Under her breath, she grumbled. "I don't understand why you would wish to do that."

At the sound of his laughter, she glowered over her shoulder at him. Elizabeth let out a small gasp at the spark of desire she felt for the native. Worse, was the realization that he knew what she had felt. More of his laughter ensued.

Elizabeth quickly washed and wrung out the peach gown. She strode over to the scout and thrust the damp garment in his lap. "I would appreciate it if you would give this to Jumping Fox. Now!"

The native's hand circled her wrist before she could move away. "You do not fear Night of Light, but you fear me. Why would that be, Elizabeth?"

"I do not know." She said as she tried to wrench herself free.

Whispering Eagle yanked her toward him, so she practically fell forward into his lap. "You have nothing to fear with me. I am your friend."

As much as his words were meant to soothe her, Elizabeth found his nearness disconcerting. "Please, let me go! I…I believe you." She stammered.

He released her abruptly, causing Elizabeth to stumble back a few steps. He threw the gown back at her. "She cannot wear this, it is wet."

Elizabeth lost her balance as she caught the dress. She landed hard on her backside. The native watched her curiously as she went into a fit of giggling.

He went over to crouch beside her, and she immediately sobered. "I went to your husband's ranch."

"You… Why?" Elizabeth was astounded.

"I took his body there." He helped her to her feet. "You need to go there. The land now belongs to you."

"I don't want to." The thought of leaving Night of Light was incomprehensible.

"We will all go with you." The scout said, as if hearing her thoughts. He waved a hand to the east. "The towns are growing closer. We need to leave this place."

"Is that why my husband was killed?" Elizabeth had to ask, but did not want to think it was true.

"Your husband was killed because Night of Light wanted you for himself." Again, as if reading her mind, he said. "He had seen you as you left the ship you were on."

"And that gave him cause to kill those people?" Elizabeth did not like this one bit.

"There is more to that meeting you had with Manny Hedder." Whispering Eagle spoke slowly. "Night of Light will have to tell you about it, when he is ready to."

Elizabeth spotted Jumping Fox, as the native woman came towards them. "Tell your sister, I said thank you for the clothing."

Without turning to look at the woman behind him, Whispering Eagle spoke a few words in his native tongue. Elizabeth waited quietly as the two conversed. Whispering Eagle eyed Elizabeth often while his sister talked. More than once, Elizabeth felt that unnerving attraction to the native scout.

After Jumping Fox left, he gave Elizabeth a long look. "She wishes she could talk to you. Her husband died in a raid, they were very close. I am gone so much, it is hard on her."

"Are you married?" Elizabeth asked, hoping to sound impersonal.

"I am not here enough to do that." He shrugged. "Each time a woman has interested me, I've had to leave. When I come back, someone else has taken her."

Whispering Eagle showed up again the next morning, as Elizabeth gathered kindling for the cooking fires. "I cannot seem to think badly of Night of Light." She glanced sideways at him. "Is that wrong?"

"He is a warrior." He waved a hand in front of his chest. "His spirit is right within himself."

Elizabeth sighed out. She felt like a jumbled mess inside. "I wish I knew myself that well."

"What has made you unsure of who you are?" Whispering Eagle took the bundle of sticks from her.

"I…ah…" Her eyes went to him, she searched his face. There was nothing the least bit encouraging in his expression. Elizabeth knew she wanted him. Her throat went dry at the thought of this. "Why do you choose to be around me so much?" She rasped out.

"I do not know." He smiled. "Have you tried on the dress Jumping Fox gave you?"

"Not yet." She thought to save it for when Night of Light returned.

"Wear it tonight." He started to walk away with his armload of kindling. "You will eat with my family."

FOUR

Elizabeth felt herself being lifted from the bed. Her arms wrapped around him as she burrowed her face into his neck. She immediately released him and began to struggle to free herself. This was not Night of Light! She was whisked out of the longhouse and set to her feet.

Her eyes narrowed on the scout. "What do you think you are doing?" She hissed out.

He grinned and watched as her angry expression turned to one of desire. He held onto her arm as two of his brothers went into the longhouse. "We are leaving tonight."

No sooner had he said that, when an arrow protruded itself into the arm of his that was furthest from her. Whispering Eagle released her to grab a mid-sized hatchet he kept at his side. He flung it into the darkness. There was a thud and then a groan, before someone fell to the forest floor. Whispering Eagle stumbled to Elizabeth. Putting her arms about him, she helped the scout regain his balance. His brothers came from the longhouse with Elizabeth's trunk of clothes.

"Leave it." She said abruptly.

"No." Whispering Eagle snarled harshly.

One of the other men went to him. In a swift move, he jerked the arrow from his brother's arm. Elizabeth tore a piece off from her dressing gown and pressed it against the wound.

They were a group of twenty that rode to the ranch. After they removed all but two of Manny Hedder's thirteen men, the natives and Elizabeth settled into the house. Whispering Eagle was near death for three days, from the infection caused by the arrow wound. Elizabeth was sitting by his bed when he first regained consciousness.

"You should be my wife." He said weakly.

"I don't think Night of Light would agree." She smiled.

"He is not here." Whispering Eagle reached out for her.

Putting her hand in his, Elizabeth leaned close. "But, he will be soon enough." Hoping she made her point.

"Yes." He rose up enough to kiss her.

It was as though electric sparks went from Elizabeth's lips to her toes. He moved his hand from hers, placing it behind her neck. Elizabeth tried to pull away, but he held steadfastly to her.

When Whispering Eagle was done, he touched his forehead to hers. "If I did not kill him."

Her eyes flickered from his bandaged arm, to his face. "That was him." She commented vaguely.

"The people who have come here with us, do not like the way he invokes the white man's wrath in these raids." He lay back against the pillow.

"But, they are invading your lands." She pointed out.

"There are too many of them." He held back the anger he felt. "We will lose more by fighting them this way."

Elizabeth could feel the hostility he tried so hard to control. "You have seen more on your excursions than Night of Light has."

The scout shook his head. "He does not understand." He gave her a half-grin. "My father said we should marry."

Elizabeth almost laughed. She liked his family. All of them spoke the native Iroquois and French. Many had also learned English. "Why would he say that?"

"He said you are the sky, the earth, and rivers combined." He reflected. "Essential to life."

"Don't you have a leader of some sort?" She didn't like where the conversation was going. Especially knowing she wanted this man.

"My father is tribal Chieftain." His eyes closed as he became weary. "I would find it hard to stay away so much, if you were my wife."

"Oh my!" Elizabeth fretted. "You certainly have trapped me here!"

"Good."

Elizabeth rose to her feet. "I will fetch you some food."

"Elizabeth," Whispering Eagle regretted the way she stiffened at his voice. "Be careful when you go outside, Night of Light may not know…"

"I told him, I would not leave of my own accord." She stared at him icily. "So he knows."

Concern filled Whispering Eagle's eyes. "Woman, don't hate me for this."

"I cannot stop you from doing what you will to me," She paused to take in an emotion filled breath. "Though you cannot decide how I will feel about it."

After she closed the door quietly behind her, Whispering Eagle muttered under his breath. "I already know how you feel. How long will you choose to deny it?"

Chief New Moon walked into the room his son was recuperating in. He shook his head slightly over the young British woman that sat near the bed in a chair. She did not see that she was in love with his son.

In the native language, he spoke. "Three times today, she has gone outside and searched out the land. She watches for him to come." He gave Elizabeth a curious look when she gazed up at him. "Does she hope for his return or dread it?"

"I do not know." Whispering Eagle answered back. In English, he asked Elizabeth, "What do you think will happen when Night of Light comes here?"

"Fighting, I suppose." Her countenance showed only trepidation. "I wish there were a better way to resolve this."

His hand went out to her and she took it. "We have tried, many times before."

"I know." She let out a long breath.

"She loves you." New Moon stated flatly. "Maybe she thinks we will not do well when we fight the others."

Elizabeth waited until the elder man left, then asked. "What did he say?"

"He told me that tomorrow they are going to get one of the town's preachers." He closed his eyes and smiled. "We will be wed in both your people and my people's ways." Whispering Eagle slowly opened his eyes. She looked as though she were trying to figure him out.

"This ranch sits on land that used to belong to your people." She stated in a blunt manner.

"Yes." His voice grew husky. It was the first show of desire he had allowed himself to show her.

"I see." She replied tersely.

Whispering Eagle winced once he realized what she thought. "It is not why I want you to be my wife."

"I think I know that." There was still tension in her voice.

He did not want to deceive her further. "If you do not want to marry me, I can stop them from bringing the preacher."

"That won't be necessary." Still, she sat stiffly.

His eyes widened at her response. "Elizabeth, my father said that you love me, that is all."

"Then you do not want to marry me." She was having a difficult time at keeping a straight face. If the charade continued much longer, Elizabeth knew she would break into hopeless laughter.

"What of Night of Light?" He asked in disbelief.

She waved a hand in the air. "He just likes to fight."

"I may have killed him, the other night in the village." He grumbled.

"He did shoot an arrow into you." She rose her chin up. "He deserves whatever beset him."

"You do not love him?" He sat forward.

"Oh yes, immensely." She now spoke on a serious note. "Though, what is this between you and I?"

"If there were to be peace between us, I think you would go back to him." It had crossed his mind and he needed to say it.

"So, am I to be a bargaining chip? A lever of some sort, to keep the peace?" She cocked a brow at him.

"Would you allow yourself to be used that way?" He countered.

"You told me you are my friend." She surmised. "If he is agreeable, maybe it would work."

"For a while." He added, a bit disappointed by this conclusion. The scout did not notice how closely she was watching him during this discussion.

A muffled giggle escaped, then full laughter took over. "I am not going back to Night of Light."

Relief flooded Whispering Eagle's face.

"If you want to get married, I will have a preacher brought." He gave her a curious look when she laughed harder. "What do you want, Elizabeth?" He asked softly.

"I want to know why I am so drawn to you." She regained a small bit of her self-control.

The native closed his mouth and shook his head. He then smiled. "Am I to send for a preacher or not?"

"Oh…" Elizabeth groaned out.

She wanted time to think, to decide. Her eyes met his hard calculating stare. Why that brought a surge of desire throughout her body, she did not know.

"Yes, bring him here."

He nodded at her, his eyes shining. "My father has had me watching the changes in the lands for many years. I was able to see what our people will need in the future."

"Then you are to become the chief?" Elizabeth wondered how she fit into the picture.

"I have other warriors. Many other warriors. I do not want Night of Light and his group back in this tribe." He flashed her a grin.

"I am carrying his child." She said astutely.

"Then he has lost that child."

Elizabeth saw no give in the scout's face. "I don't know if I can do that." She almost whispered.

"You agreed to be my wife, and to allowing the tribe to move to your lands. Is there some reason you want him in the child's life?" He tested his arm and found it quite sore. "I will be taking over as chief once we are married. I wish you would talk to me about what you need."

"We can work this out as we both see what needs to be done." Elizabeth was the one to give in. "I think for the present, I will do as you suggest."

His head came up sharply and he eyed her a moment. "I think you have lost your fear of me."

"Yes, I have." Her body came to tingling life as his gaze went over her.

He smiled leisurely. "I had not expected you to be so beautiful."

Elizabeth had no idea what he meant by that.

Two days after their conversation, a local preacher was brought to Whispering Eagle's bedside. The marriage certificate was signed by Father Protts in an informal ceremony. The true festivities would be a week later, in the style of a Mohawk wedding.

FIVE

After a long prayer by New Moon, the couple received baskets of food and cloth fabrics. Elizabeth now saw that there were many more people than those that had originally come with them to the ranch. To the northeast of the property, a longhouse was being built.

On the top of a large hill in the distance, a group of twelve men sat on horseback. That property was not part of the ranch's landholdings. Elizabeth's gaze stopped there.

Her hand went under the table to her new husband's thigh. "Whispering Eagle."

Her touch seared him, and he had to fight for his own restraint. "Woman, I am trying to wait until the celebration is over."

"He's watching." She said quietly.

He took her hand, bringing it up to the table. "They have been there since this morning." The scout nodded toward the east and west. Two groups, having sixteen men each, were waiting for Night of Light and his men to approach. "We are ready for him."

A hand dug into Elizabeth's shoulder, causing her to twist around on the bench where she was sitting. She was lifted up from her seat. "Those are Mohicans, She Wolf." His eyes went dangerously to Whispering Eagle. They are ready for you. It is time for you to become chieftain."

"Let go of my wife." Whispering Eagle spoke smoothly, yet there was no doubt of the threat in his voice.

"Oh God!" Elizabeth pointed to where the men on horseback had sat.

There were at least fifty riders now coming toward them. The area became a mad scrambling of men running to get weapons and horses. Elizabeth, Night of Light, and Whispering Eagle stood in the midst of this.

"Let me fight for our people." The warrior still had a grip on Elizabeth. When Whispering Eagle gave a slight nod, Night of Light shoved Elizabeth away from him.

Whispering Eagle's arm came around her. He kissed her neck. "Go to my father."

She ran over to where New Moon and many others stood together. The elder grinned just barely, as a war cry went up among the Mohawks.

It was bloody and savage the way they fought. Elizabeth could not believe that what she was watching would be considered a war. War was supposed to be thought out, calculated and organized. Not this chaotic random attack.

One of the Mohawk children was snatched up by one of the Mohican riders. Elizabeth could do nothing, it was too far away from where she stood. She tried to call out to one of the warriors, but she went unheard over the whooping calls of the fighting men.

Elizabeth finally had seen enough to understand the danger she and her small group were in. She maneuvered New Moon and the few others around them toward the house. At the very least, it would spare them from the possibility of a random arrow hitting one of them.

She was mortified by this insane conflict. She put the chief and natives in the kitchen. There, they could still see the combat and know if they needed to evacuate further, maybe even leave the ranch property.

Elizabeth went through the house, looking for places they could remain safe, if that was even a probable circumstance. In the largest of the bedrooms, she kept thinking that something seemed odd. Not seeing what it was, she crossed the floor to leave the room. She felt a small victory as she again strode through the bedroom. The floor sounded hollow underneath her feet. Elizabeth pushed the rug away and sure enough, there was a door cut into the floorboards.

It took her quite a few minutes to convince the natives to move from the kitchen into the hidden cellar. New Moon flat out refused. He was still chief until the ritual was performed with Whispering Eagle.

It was just the two of them looking out the back window, when New Moon pointed to something on the left. "My eyes are fading."

Elizabeth peered at what he may have seen. "Those are some of the warriors that ride with Night of Light."

"Hmm. What are they doing?"

"They are fighting." She looked at the elder man. "Had I missed what you had seen?"

"Where is Night of Light? He is supposed to fight with them."

They both scanned the ongoing battle. Neither could find the warrior. Elizabeth felt as though a rock had pitted itself in her stomach. New Moon took the missing warrior as a bad sign.

"We need to get some of our wounded into the ground where they will be safe." He nodded back toward the bedroom where the other natives were hidden.

"I will see if there are others out there to help." Elizabeth volunteered.

Her hair was grabbed and she was yanked back so hard, her feet flew out from under her. Night of Light stood over her, his hands clenched into fists. Elizabeth was sure he was going to beat her. The warrior gave the old chief a rigid glare, then gabbed Elizabeth by the arm and whipped her onto his shoulder.

Once outside the house, he put her on his horse and jumped up behind her. She thought he would take off with her, to someplace that they wouldn't be found. But, he headed them right into the fighting. Elizabeth was much surprised that both the Mohawks and the Mohicans moved out of their way.

"What are you doing?" She hissed back at him.

"Whispering Eagle has fallen, we need to get him out of here." His mouth touched the back of her neck. "They will not attack you."

"Why?" She had many more questions, but this was all she could think to ask in her stunned state.

"They think we are holding you captive." He chuckled quietly. "When we get Whispering Eagle back to the house, you and I will be leaving."

"I..." She started to cry. "I don't know what to do."

"You are doing just fine, She Wolf."

She heard the murmurs among the Mohicans. Night of Light waved his warriors over to where Whispering Eagle lay on the ground. One of the natives lifted him to another one on horseback. The group rode to the house.

Elizabeth glanced back at Night of Light. "You said that to me so they would see me upset."

"Yes." But when she tried to dismount his horse, he held her there.

"I thought you said…?" She searched his face, but his expression was hidden.

"I wouldn't have said it to you otherwise, She Wolf." He kicked his horse's flanks. "Manny Hedder had been a friend of mine. This land I sold to him." He continued riding away from the house, the fighting. His warriors followed, not far behind. "We used to talk often together. He told me of the women that could be brought here from England. I asked him to send out for one, for me. I do not write good English. What you read in those letters were from me, not him. We will reach my ranch in three days."

Elizabeth began crying. She had been deceived, but not by this man – the man she had almost hurt. "Are you angry with me?"

"No." Then after a moment he said. "I did not know that he had used his own name. When he had read those few letters from you, I just did not know. I should have told you that first day."

"I love you Night of Light." She felt strong in that truth.

"Good, I would hate to have to kill my brother for stealing you." He grinned when she looked back at him. "Do not worry, he was simply a proxy for me when the preacher came. You are my wife."

Elizabeth let out a breath. "I feel foolish."

He laughed. "You have done nothing foolish." His mouth came down on hers briefly. "I love you, She Wolf."

Wandering Hearts

PRELUDE

Twenty-Two Years Earlier

The carriage raced around the bend just as two shots were fired. The driver and his son fell lifeless to the ground. Marriss Calhoun tried to stop her husband and brother from leaving the coach, regardless of how well armed they were. And now, they too had been killed.

The highwaymen hooted and hollered as they brought the trunk off of the top cargo compartment. Two of the men noticed her inside. One of those grabbed Marriss's arm and began pulling her out. She reached quickly behind herself to open the latch on the other door. Flinging the portal wide, she shoved at the small boy who had hidden close to her back.

"Run!" She screamed at the child. "God, please run!"

Either the bandits didn't hear her, or more likely they didn't care about the fate of a young lad. Five year old Jeremy Calhoun quickly obeyed his mother's frantic cries. Barely understanding what was happening, yet thoroughly frightened, he fled into the woods. Never looking back, he did not stop until his little legs gave out. Wearily he crumpled barely conscious to the hard earth.

After looting the coach, the highwaymen took the goods and the screaming woman far into the hills. For three days, they abused and had their way with her. Tired of their play, they dumped her outside of a small village, barely alive.

Eight and a half months later, Marriss gave birth to a child in her father's home. Since his daughter had not recovered from the ordeal, Mitchell Howsing took it into his own hands to deal with this grandchild of his. His understanding of it was, that it was not a product of Marriss's marriage. He rid the household of the only living reminder of the horrifying incident. Mitchell's highly paid solicitor had no qualms removing the babe from the Howsing's presence. Marriss never saw the child, being told it had died at birth.

Banns were posted in a great effort to find the missing Jeremy Calhoun. There were a few false reports and possible sightings, but none of it panned out. Marriss Calhoun died six months later. She had simply given up hope.

ONE

The leaves were just turning brown along the edges, as the weather still fluctuated between the warmth and coolness of early autumn. Birds sang, seemingly undisturbed by the rider on the well-muscled bay gelding.

She sat ramrod stiff until reaching the bottom of the hill, which obscured her from the view of the manor house. Relaxing now, her body leaned forward to become one with the horse, as together they raced beside the woodland.

Charity Hatters Pinron needed to expel some of her energy before frustration completely took over her thoughts. After a two year engagement and three and a half weeks of marriage, she had yet to know the intimacy of her bridal bed.

Oh, it was not her dearest Caswell's fault. The injury happened the day before he was to leave his military position, just five days before they were to be married. After much discussion, they decided to go through with the nuptials. Though, the honeymoon would have to wait.

Charity was mulling over why it couldn't have been an arm instead of his hip that had been broken. A bright color in the trees caught her eye. Panic caused her to rein the bay too fast. He reared up, tossing Charity to the ground. As if sensing his error, the gelding cautiously went to where Charity now lay.

The entire left side of her body seemed incapable of movement, the pain was excruciating. A moment of struggle got her up on her one good foot. She hopped to the horse and after much effort, was able to get her left foot in the stirrup. Gripping the mane in her right hand, she tugged. Charity let out a yelp as pain shot up her leg. Gritting her teeth as tears ran down her cheeks, she threw herself onto the gelding's back.

Five men in brightly colored clothing, rode out of the trees. One stopped and nodded to her. The other four quickly surrounded Charity's horse. She did not need to be told where they came from. They obviously belonged to one of the wandering bands of Gypsies that plagued the countryside. Her hand reached quickly for the reins.

"Bring her off of the horse." The lone man commanded.

Before she could react, the men had dismounted and pulled her down. One man slung her right arm over his shoulder while putting his own arm around her waist. She half hopped and was half carried to the man who seemed to be in charge.

Once she was in front of him, he stared hard into her eyes. "You are injured."

Why she felt a twinge of guilt from his blunt statement, Charity did not know. Her chin jutted out defensively. "I had seen something in the trees that had frightened me. So, if I am hurt, it's your fault."

He crossed his arms over his massive chest as he looked down at her. His face though, relaxed into a grin. "Me? You are blaming me?"

"You are trespassing on land that belongs to my husband and myself." She countered with ebbing anger. My but he was a handsome specimen. "If I had not seen you, this would not have happened." His dark eyes had literally captured hers. She had to take a breath before continuing. "If you could kindly have your men help me back on my horse. I must return home and seek medical care."

"We will take you back to your house." He watched as she paled. Did he frighten her that much?

"No, you can't…"

It was a good thing that the Gypsy man named Mihai still held her, when she fainted dead away. "I will take her home."

"No." Shandor said quickly. "She was right in telling me that we can't." When Mihai narrowed his eyes, Shandor clarified. "If she goes into a delirium, she may blame us."

"Then what do we do?" Asked the one whose name was Emilian. His eyes went over the woman. She was pretty, for an Englishwoman.

Shandor mounted his horse. "Hand her up to me. We will ask Walther what to do."

"But our encampment is far on the other side of the village!" Emilian envisioned the woman's husband hunting them down for the return of his wife.

Mihai was in his saddle and already holding the reins to the gelding. "That's possible." He chuckled. "If Bo hasn't moved it yet."

<u>TWO</u>

When Charity's eyes opened, she felt sleepy. Her eyelids in fact, refused to stay open more than a crack and then only for seconds at a time. It was moments later, when a hardened muscular body lay completely over top of hers. She could feel the strong evidence of his manhood. Where that particular member pushed up against her body, caused her to moan out.

"This should not take long." A vaguely familiar voice said quietly in her ear.

His arms clasped her tightly to him. She moaned out again as desire swept through her. A garbled scream came from her as pain invaded her left shoulder. After a moment, only a dull ach existed there. Her peace was not to last, as it was now her leg that made her cry out in agony. That too, slowly changed into only a mild discomfort.

"No!" Softly escaped her lips as he started to slide off of her.

"You need rest." He whispered.

Charity was left alone in the darkness, yearning for something she had yet to experience. She awoke again, to voices speaking quietly nearby.

"He had allowed her to go out that far, unescorted."

"He's hurt." Saying those two words drained Charity completely of energy. A cool wet cloth was placed on her forehead.

"Shh." Florica said, while glancing at the man sitting on the other side of the English woman. "Come talk with me outside." Walther followed his daughter out of the canvas tent.

This left Shandor alone with Charity. "You are at our camp. Your arm and leg had come out of joint. We fixed both." He studied her form, seeing no indication that she had heard him.

"When...?" She asked in a breath.

"You have been here three days."

Her eyes flew open, then drooped wearily. "I...ah...oh." Charity was too exhausted to speak, or even think.

"I will return later."

She did not hear or see him leave. It was more that she sensed that he was no longer there.

"We are making the move tomorrow." Walther said to the group as they sat around the fire, sharing the evening meal. His eyes grazed over everyone, stopping on the young lady seated between his daughter and Shandor. "Will you be coming with us?"

Charity smiled. She truly liked the elder man, for all his strange secretive ways. "No. I believe it is past due for me to return to my husband."

Walther's gaze went to his wife, who sat beside him. "Danka, is there anything to be said?"

The wizened woman peered at the cards that she had slowly set before herself. "The marriage is incomplete." She stared knowingly at Charity. "She does not know him as a woman should know her husband."

A dark stain of blush rose high on Charity's cheeks. "I...ah...we..." She rose up and quickly ran into the forest surrounding the camp.

Shandor got to his feet just as fast, to chase after her. He found her sitting on an overturned tree, trembling. "Is it the shock of her accuracy, or did what she say upset you?"

Charity shook her head. "My husband was injured just before our wedding. So, we've had to wait." Her eyes teared up as her voice shook a little. "I appreciate what all of you have done for me. I have to go back now, he must be terribly worried."

Shandor sat down beside her, covering her hand with his. "Your marriage is not legal until it is consummated." When she looked up at him, his mouth covered hers. His tongue forcefully parted her lips to heatedly claim her.

Charity's hands went to his shoulders, to shove him away. "No! I can't!"

Shandor's hand gripped onto her wrist. She gasped after taking one look at his eyes. Searching her mind for an argument that would appease this man of what he planned to do to her, she could find nothing.

"Please, don't!" She finally pleaded.

He took her hand and kissed the palm of it. Sensuously his tongue lingered from one finger to the next. He grinned warmly before releasing her. "Come with us. You can always go back there if you wish to. Though, you may never have the chance to leave again."

"She's not going anywhere with you."

They both looked up at the voice. Jonathan Pinron stood with one hand on his hip. In the other hand, he held a gun which was aimed at the Gypsy man.

"Jon, don't!" Charity put herself between the two men. "I had injured myself when I fell from my horse. Before I could tell them where to take me, I went unconscious."

Jonathan still was wary, though he put his gun back in its holster. "Then I was in error. I'll take you back home to my brother." He put a hand out to her, then his eyes widened.

Charity looked at her side when she felt something jab into her ribs. Her gaze went from the gun Shandor pointed at her, slowly up to his eyes. "Why are you doing this?"

He refused to look at her. Instead, his stare remained on the Englishman. "We are owed for medical care for this woman. No less than two hundred pounds."

Fear for Charity and shock came over Jonathan. "I do not carry that much money on me and the bank is closed for two more days!"

"Then bring it here on Monday." Shandor's free hand covered Charity's mouth. "She will remain safe with us until then."

Jonathan stood there a moment, unsure of what to do. He had no other men with him. They had all been sent to search to the east, which was in the opposite direction of the manor than he had gone. He remembered the inn he had passed in the village. His gaze stayed on the Gypsy, though the words were meant for Charity. "I will be staying in a room at Rippley's Tavern." He turned and walked the course that would take him back to where he left his horse.

"I think we should leave tonight." Walther said, coming up behind them.

"He will follow." Shandor put his gun away.

"Then he will be gravely disappointed when he finds neither of you with us." Walther chuckled at his own plan. "We will see you at the new grounds in a month's time." His sharp eyes affixed on Charity. "Both of you." He started to walk away. "And take Hanzi with you. He has been restless of late."

After the ancient Gypsy disappeared into his wagon, Shandor faced Charity. He dreaded this, for he knew she would be hostile towards him, at the very least. But, when she looked up into his eyes, there was something very different there. Some unknown emotion.

"Who is Hanzi?" Charity almost laughed at the look of jealousy he put forth.

THREE

Charity watched for an opportunity to escape as the two men packed what they could on the three horses. The problem was that her gelding was one of them, they were strapping things to. Also, it seemed as though one of the Gypsies always had Charity in sight. She sighed in resignation as Donka sat down by her.

"I will tell your fortune." The older woman said. Her wrinkled face creased further when she smiled.

Charity nodded. At least it would take her mind off of her problems. She picked three cards from the spread out deck, as Donka had told her to do.

Donka's eyes lit with glee as the first card she turned revealed a tiger. "There is much power in the man who loves you. But, he is not what you think. There is a deception surrounding him, it involves him personally." Her eyes went to Charity and intensified. "Your own power is growing and you will need it to save this man one day."

"Do I love him?" Charity asked innocently.

Donka shrugged as she turned over the next card. It was a woman wearing a white gown standing in a shallow stream. Tucked in one arm was a book. Her other hand stretched out toward a large star above her.

Donka's eyes widened at this one and she let out a small gasp. "You look for logic in life and that is what you live by." Her head nodded slightly. "But you truly wish for those things that do not abide by reason." She stared at Charity as though stunned. "Your strength is in your heart. The power you need is found only through your love." She quickly went to the next card. It was a man lifting an injured ox onto his shoulders.

"Is that the man who loves me?" Charity knew she was getting too caught up in the woman's storytelling. But, it was interesting to hear.

As Shandor strolled towards them, Donka put the deck back together and set them to her side. "You must help him. For the burden he carries is…" She became silent in Shandor's presence.

"Walther told me to ask you for extra blankets." Again, he avoided looking at Charity. He grinned none-the-less. She would be near for at least a while longer.

"Yes, I will bring them to you." Rising to her feet, she quickly said to Charity. "It is something only you can or will be able to do." With a slight limp, she made her way to one of the wagons.

"Pick a card from the deck." Shandor said with a devilish grin.

"I already did." Charity replied flippantly. "Three, to be exact."

He let out a short laugh. "This will be different, I promise."

"Alright." Charity let out an exaggerated breath as she plucked a card from the middle of the deck. It was blank, absolutely nothing on it.

Shandor crouched down. Flipping the entire deck over, he spread the cards out. They were all as empty as the one Charity drew. "Now pick one."

She did hesitantly. "Oh!"

On it was a waterfall with two cherubs playing in it. A man was on one side, holding a hand out to a woman who seemed to be reaching for him.

Charity couldn't stop herself as she giggled childishly. She picked another card, then another. They were all the same as the first.

Shandor took the first card she had drawn. He tucked it in a pouch attached to his wide belt. After gathering the cards together, he placed them back where Donka had left them.

"They do different things every time." He explained.

"Aren't you going to pick one?" Charity was now most curious as to what his card would be.

"I have." He replied casually. "And it is always the same." He rose, putting a hand out to her.

Allowing him to help her up, she asked, "And what would that be?"

Before he could answer, Donka arrived with the blankets. Within minutes, they were ready to go.

Charity almost regretted her plans for escape as Shandor lifted her onto the gelding's back. It was not even a choice to be made, she had to get back to her life. The inn that Jonathan mentioned, let her know precisely where she was. It was the last tavern on the northeast road that led out of the village.

They had just ridden out of sight of the encampment, when Shandor rode up beside her. "I don't want to have to chase you down." He pulled her from the saddle, placing her in front of him on his horse.

She looked back at him, but refused to say anything. If she acted as though she had any thoughts on leaving, he would never trust her enough so she could escape.

Charity sucked in a breath when his hand dropped to her inner thigh. He rubbed his thumb almost absently against her. After several tense minutes, she found herself taking short gasping breaths. His hand moved up her thigh, where it stopped sent explosions of pleasure through her. Charity cried out lightly as his hand went from that soft mound then to other sensitive areas, before massaging her breasts. She leaned back against Shandor, her hands gripping his muscled upper legs. He brought her to endless pinnacles that left her panting.

Abruptly he stopped and slowed his horse. "We will camp here for the night."

<u>**FOUR**</u>

Charity sat on a boulder watching as the two Gypsy men made bedrolls from the thick woolen blankets. It wasn't until Shandor came to get her that she realized the chance she had missed. The horses were staked not more than two strides from where she had been sitting. Her mind had been so caught up on the new wondrous feelings that Shandor had elicited in her that she had not even noticed until the moment had passed.

As soon as she was under the blankets, Shandor began undressing her. Charity wanted to fight him, but found it impossible. Every time he removed an article of her clothing, his mouth replaced the discarded item. She became lost in the sensations and was clutching him to her as his naked body came over her likewise bared flesh.

She felt the heat of him as he pushed against her virginal boundary. Charity had a moment of clarity as he entered her warm folds.

She softly cried. "No!" Just as Shandor tore through her maidenhead.

He held her head to his chest, feeling the wetness of her tears. Laying Charity gently back down, he moved slowly out of her. She almost purred as the delightful ambiances replaced the pain of mere seconds before.

His mouth caught hers as he moved more surely within her moist tight body. When Shandor felt the first grips of her ecstasy, he slowed down but drove in deeply. Then with sudden urgency, he sped up. Charity's legs wrapped around his back as she desperately clung to him through one orgasm, then another. As she went into her third flight, he expelled himself within her. It was only minutes of rest when he went after her again.

He and Hanzi had allowed her to sneak off late that night. Shandor wanted her to go to this *husband* of hers, armed with the knowledge of the invalidity of their marriage among other things.

When she had come out of the inn with Jonathan, she had acted as though the lovemaking of the previous night had never happened. Shandor made a low guttural growl in his throat, causing Hanzi to look at him in concern.

Shandor's knuckles turned white as he gripped his horse's reins while trying to control the seething rage inside of him. But then, she turned her face away from Jonathan to hide the tear she wiped from her cheek.

The few glimpses Shandor caught of her as they rode toward the manor, gave him cause to worry. She had become increasingly pale and he wondered if she might faint. From the trees, he and Hanzi observed as Charity and Jonathan stopped along the road. Jonathan helped Charity dismount from the gelding. She went running toward some bushes, where she immediately vomited.

Hanzi glanced over at Shandor, with a raised brow. "How far are you going to let her take this?"

Shandor couldn't keep the beaming grin from his face. "As long as it takes her to realize that she has something that belongs to me."

It was five miles further up the road, that the first shot was fired. Shandor kicked his stallion, urging him to run. The lover's quarrel between him and Charity was put to a quick ending.

It took a full night of riding for Charity to reach the village and locate Rippley's Tavern. She roused Jonathan and by eight that morning they were half the way to the manor. That is when the shot rang out. Charity turned in her saddle in time to see Jonathan fall off of his horse. She had no further time to think as Shandor raced up on his deep russet colored stallion.

"Not our doing." He said, scooping her off of her horse and placing her neatly in front of him. "I promise."

Just as they made it to the trees, another retort was heard. The bullet whizzed by them, embedding in a nearby sapling.

"Hanzi will get your friend to the closest house."

"If they don't shoot him as well." Charity added, her voice sounding shaky at best.

"They were shooting at you." He grimaced, thinking afterward that he shouldn't have said that so bluntly. Turning now in the direction of the village, he asked. "Who are you?"

"Charity Hatters Pinron." She spoke barely loud enough to be heard. "I know of no reason for someone to try to harm me."

"Pinron?" Well I do." Actually, Shandor knew quite a lot about that family name.

"If you plan to slander my husband..." Charity tensed.

"He is not your husband as of yet." Shandor grinned. "And no, I have no ill thoughts towards the Pinron family, but there are others who do."

At dusk, they were back at the campsite where they had stayed the previous evening. Shandor explained that they were to wait for Hanzi. From there, the three of them would ride to catch up with Wather and the others. Jonathan no longer posed a threat to them.

Seeing how tired Charity was, Shandor put the blanket down for her to sleep. He watched her as weariness took her into slumber. His mind went back to the day she had fallen off of the horse. Had the person who shot Jonathan been watching her that day as well? If they hadn't taken her injured body to the Gypsy camp, she may very well not be alive today.

Hanzi came up next to Shandor silently. "I had to go to three different homes to get him help." At Shandor's questioning look, he waved a hand at his own clothing. "I do not think they like us much." He then grinned. "The third place belonged to a doctor. He was a nice man."

Shandor cast a doubtful look at his friend. Hanzi had no great love for the British. "Nice?"

Hanzi chuckled. "He is from Spain. The man told me that my clothing reminded him of his homeland." His eyes went to where Charity lay. "I had to knock that man unconscious." He shrugged. "He pulled his gun out when I was trying to get him back on his horse."

"He may have thought you meant him harm." Shandor replied.

"Then why would I have stopped to help him?" Anger flashed in the Gypsy's eyes. "I had told him as much, when I was lifting him onto his saddle."

"Englishmen!" Shandor spat out bitterly. "I think they have no sense sometimes."

After a bit of silence between them, Hanzi spoke. "I never did see who was shooting at them."

"Whoever it was, had been shooting at her." Then it hit Shandor. "Or maybe they were trying to get at her, by killing her protectors."

A sudden laugh shook Hanzi's shoulders. "What if it was one of the men her husband sent to find her?"

Both men found much humor in that. In fact, they guffawed so loudly that it woke Charity.

"What has the two of you laughing so?" She listened as Hanzi related his theory about the shooter. After a moment, she shook her head. "That's not possible. All of Caswell's men know Jonathan. He is at the manor more often than he is at his own home. Most likely, he is the one in charge of the search for me."

"I am taking you to Walther and the others." Shandor questioned the smile that came to her face, despite her effot to hide it. "Then I am going to go talk to Jonathan Pinron. Maybe he knows why this happened."

"Then he is going to be alright?" Relief showed on her face.

"He was strong enough to try to fight me, when I lent aid to him." Hanzi replied tersely.

"Then why bother going?" Her eyes went to Shandor with the inquiry.

"Well, I thought…" His brow furrowed as he tried to understand why she had asked that question. "In case you try to go back…"

"Nonsense!" Charity waved a hand in the air. "It would be totally improper of me to return to Caswell in…ah…"

Shandor's eyes widened as he grinned. "Hmm?"

"Oh!" She gave him a look of disgust. "You wretched man! You've planted your seed and now I am going to have your child!"

"You don't think your *Caswell* would understand?" He sneered out the other man's name, as he became frustrated with her reaction to the baby she carried.

"It wouldn't be right. This is not Caswell's responsibility. The child is yours and mine." Her eyes went downward, then looked up at Shandor pleadingly. "I wanted what we did last night to happen. Please! Don't cast me and our child aside!"

Shandor crouched down in front of Charity. He lightly brushed the tears that had started falling down her cheeks. "I would never put you or any children we may have, away from me." His voice was quiet and soothing.

What she had said made him feel every bit of the man he was. He still did not trust her to not run off. His world was very different than what she was used to. Shandor was more than sure that it frightened her, which meant that at any time she could take flight.

He stared into her eyes. "We should go now."

Hanzi had already left the couple alone, he now returned with the horses. Charity rode with Shandor, as Hanzi led her bay beside his own mount. They traveled until early evening. All three of them went to sleep as soon as they brought the blankets out.

<u>FIVE</u>

Caswell Pinron handed the letter over to the barrister. What Charity had written on it was an explanation and an apology over the events that had happened to her.

The barrister's expression turned to shock as he read over the part about the shooting. He set the letter down on Caswell's bedside table. "What would you have me do?"

"Grant her an annulment as quickly as possible." He had received the letter almost two weeks ago and had resigned himself to his decision.

Barrister Thompson scoffed openly. "Perhaps this is a mere infatuation for her. I mean really! A Gypsy!"

"Charity is one of the most level-headed people I know." Caswell smiled at the thought of her. "We have been friends for too long. This is something else for her, something special."

"Alright then." The portly man rose with much effort. "I will start the proceedings."

Jonathan entered the room as the official took his leave. "You have settled it then?" He was concerned for his brother and doubted that ending the marriage was the best decision for him.

"Yes." He looked over at his younger sibling. "I am thinking strongly about going back into the service. Since I've been stuck in this bed, I have thought about it quite often."

"Had you mentioned that to Charity?" Jonathan thought maybe this was the reason she had chosen to stay away.

Caswell's eyes went wide in mock horror. "By the Saints! I would never have done that!"

"Then why do you think she does not want to come back?" It made no sense to Jonathan.

"Perhaps fear of another attack…" He hesitated a moment, then added more quietly, "I think she might be with-child." He could see rage in his brother's face. "Jonathan, she was not forced. I have known Charity for too long. I would be most aware if something was wrong."

"But what of the property?"

"I thought you could look after it." He laughed as his brother's eyes bulged out. "Oh that. Yes well, she suggested that since both of our money had been invested in it, to divide the money from the horse breeding." He laughed some more. "As well as the manor house."

"You're going to sell?" Jonathan was incredulous over this.

"No, of course not." Caswell was quite amused by the whole thing. "I'm taking the west wing, since I'm already settled here. And she'll take the east wing." He sobered slightly. "We're going to be partners, only in business instead of life."

"What are you going to do when she brings that band of Gypsies here?" He asked with a sneer of distaste.

"Treat them cordially, as it would be with any guest. Did I mention that if it weren't for one of those Gypsies, you seem to think dreadful," He shifted in the bed with hopes of gaining some comfort before continuing. "That I, dear brother, may have breathed my last in that field where we encountered those cattle thieves."

"This is the first you have told me of it." Jonathan felt his lack of worldliness as his brother recanted the story of what happened when he was finally making his trip home.

"It was purely by mistake." The older Pinron brother continued. "That we had the misfortune of coming upon those thieves…"

During the ride, Charity listened to a version of the same story. Shandor and Hanzi took turns in the telling of the encounter when they rescued the British troops.

"We found five of them that had gotten stampeded." Shandor explained.

Hanzi nodded as he rode beside them. "I went to find a doctor while Shandor, Bo, and Emilian kept the cattle from doing further damage."

"I wonder how many of them lived after that." Shandor mused.

And, if they even know what had happened to them." Hanzi added. "It was an awful thing to see."

"At least all the men who caused it got caught." After seeing the anger burn in Hanzi's eyes, Shandor wished he had left out that part of the story.

"It was almost us who got blamed." Hanzi glanced at Charity. He refrained from verbalizing his dislike for the English. "One soldier stopped them from locking us up."

Shandor laughed out a bit of the nervousness caused by the memory. "He called out to the constable, *'Those men are with us'* and then he passed out." He gave Hanzi a stern look. "Now there is an Englishman that can be trusted."

"Do you have many problems with the people here in Britain?" Charity thought to ask.

That question brought new stories, about the good and bad treatment of Gypsies. Many of the tales were about England, but there were also ones in other parts of Europe. The conversation turned to the abuses the Europeans laid to the Gypsy women. Shandor's arm tightened protectively over Charity's abdomen.

Charity's mind went to other things that she had picked up on during the discussion. First, was the fierce temperament of the Gypsy men when their jealousy became peaked. And second, that it did not take much to cause that jealously to show up. Charity had always heard how loose the morals of the Gypsy people were. Now, she was sure that the information had been wrong.

After several days of travel, Charity thought they seemed to be going in circles. When she vocalized her thoughts, both men laughed. Indeed they were, though it was more of a spiral that they rode in. The middle point was where they were to re-unite with Walther's band of Gypsies.

SIX

Each night Shandor made love to her passionately and lovingly. One evening, there was a twinge of brutality added to it. He did not hurt her, but had been rough to the point of punishing. During it, Charity had wondered why he was so angry at her. Afterwards as he held her, he had been so gentle that her body responded with more sensitivity to his touch. This quickly rose her to a peak and he took her again.

Shandor had been overly restless that night. He had paced while Hanzi and Charity finished the sparse meal of the rabbit that had been caught and cooked over the campfire. An hour was spent checking over the horses, for the next few days would be filled with rugged riding. Shandor then walked off into the darkness.

It was an hour before daylight when he returned to the bedroll made out for Charity and himself. Shandor could not relax any better than he had earlier. The horses had acted strangely, as though something or someone were near. He had searched the grounds surrounding the camp, but found nothing to verify the sense of trepidation he felt. It wasn't until Hanzi rose for the day, that sleep finally came to Shandor.

Hanzi and Charity ate a brief repast of hard biscuits as Shandor slept. Though neither of them spoke of it, there was an eerie caution that hung in the air. Then the sound of a twig breaking, and a low throaty voice. Was it man or beast? Hanzi motioned for Charity to stay where she was as he silently rose to his feet.

The Gypsy was shot in his left shoulder. He purposely fell to the ground, pulling Charity flat in the dirt beside him. Now very awake, Shandor rolled over by them.

He brought his gun out as he leaned over Hanzi. "How bad is it?"

"I can still shoot."

Charity tugged on Shandor's arm. "He…he's…!"

Shandor looked up to see a man coming toward them. It was like looking at his own reflection in a pond of water. A bit warbled, but close enough to pass for an image of himself. The man brought his gun up and aimed.

Hanzi shot three times into the invader. He didn't care who the man was, he had been about to kill Shandor. He glanced over at his friend. "A relative of yours?"

Shandor shrugged unconvincingly. "I wouldn't know."

Charity stared at the man, now lying dead. "He must be." Her eyes went to Shandor. "Do you know if he could be…?"

"No, I have never seen any of my family, to my recollection."

Hanzi winced as Florica removed the bullet from his arm. "I may need something." He said through clenched teeth.

Walther handed him a bottle that contained a liquor that he made himself. "Shandor should drink some of this as well. He seems to have something bothering him of late."

"He didn't tell you what happened?" Hanzi wondered.

"No, as soon as he got you here, he and that woman took off." He grumbled out. "Danka said it was something that they needed to do. That woman forever keeps me in suspense."

Florica laughed quietly. "You are not the only one she does that to." She looked up, ready to expose a secret. "Mama said that one of her cards came up missing."

"Maybe that is why this has transpired." Walther stared a moment at Hanzi. "So, what did happen with the three of you out there?"

Hanzi looked down from the table he sat on and stared at his feet. "The man who shot me, had to be a relative of Shandor's. There was barely any difference between them. I don't think Shandor could shoot him because of that."

Walther thought long on this. "Was it necessary to kill the man?"

"It would have been Shandor who was dead if I didn't stop the man. I could see it in his eyes." Hanzi shook his head a bit. "Then we had to have Charity bring a constable while we hid in the woods."

Walther had a shocked expression on his face. "How did she explain being out there by herself?"

The younger man smiled. "She told them her horse had gone into a run and she couldn't control it."

Walther laughed. "So she will be returning when Shandor comes back to us?"

"Yes, he peaked her interest about our life." Hanzi could see that the band's leader didn't believe his story. "And, she is going to have Shandor's baby."

Walther walked away from Hanzi and his daughter feeling light at heart. Other than the shooting, good things were happening.

Charity had stopped by to see the constable about the man who had been shot. As she had thought, the official had checked into the assailant. He sat her down at the jail to talk with her about the man.

"He was a product of rape. His mother was Marriss Calhoun, although her husband was not the father. Old Howsing, Marriss's father had gotten rid of the child. He had hoped to find Jeremy Calhoun, who had been his legitimate grandson. Well, that hasn't happened in all these years and now Mitch Howsing is not going to be around much longer."

"That's why he was shooting at us." She surmised aloud.

"Who? I thought you said you had been alone." He gave her a suspicious look.

"Tell me, did Jeremy disappear when he was very young?" She ask in her no-nonsense tone.

"He was around five years old. Why?" He now became interested.

"I know where he is."

SEVEN

The nurse took them up the grand winding staircase and through the marbled floor second story hall. At the last door, she stopped and turned to the couple.

"The *other one* had come here once." She said quietly. "He had caused quite an uproar and Mr. Howsing had a heart-attack. Apparently, that *man* found out that he would inherit if you couldn't be found."

Shandor looked at Charity, taking her hand. "So, we had guessed."

The door was opened for them and they walked in. To their surprise, Mitchell Howsing was not in the bed. Instead, he stood staring out the windows of his room.

"Mr. Howsing, your grandson Jeremy has come home."

He turned to face them and tears fell from his eyes. "Thank God you're alive!" Mitch walked over and embraced the man. As he did, he whispered non-to-quietly in his grandson's ear. "Isn't that Caswell Pinron's woman?"

Shandor laughed as he took a step back. "I'll tell you about it someday, Grandfather." He gave the older man a sweeping glance. "You know what? I remember you."